Bushwhackers Bushwhacked!

When they came within hailing distance of the cabin, Win held up his hand and started to call out, but before he could do so, a puff of smoke erupted from the window, followed by the sound of a rifle shot. A single bullet took off his hat.

"Hey! Hold on there!" Win shouted. "We don't mean you—"

The rifle fired a second time, this time hitting Joe's horse. The animal, struck in the heart, went down so quickly that Joe just managed to leap clear.

"Stop shooting, you son of a bitch!" Win shouted.

DON'T MISS THESE
ALL-ACTION WESTERN SERIES
FROM THE BERKLEY PUBLISHING GROUP

THE GUNSMITH by J. R. Roberts
Clint Adams was a legend among lawmen, outlaws, and ladies. They called him . . . the Gunsmith.

LONGARM by Tabor Evans
The popular long-running series about U.S. Deputy Marshal Long—his life, his loves, his fight for justice.

SLOCUM by Jake Logan
Today's longest-running action Western. John Slocum rides a deadly trail of hot blood and cold steel.

BUSHWHACKERS by B. J. Lanagan
An all-new series by the creators of Longarm! The rousing adventures of the most brutal gang of cutthroats ever assembled—Quantrill's Raiders.

BUSHWHACKERS

THE KILLING EDGE

B. J. Lanagan

JOVE BOOKS, NEW YORK

THE KILLING EDGE

A Jove Book / published by arrangement with
the author

PRINTING HISTORY
Jove edition / November 1997

The Putnam Berkley World Wide Web site address is
http://www.berkley.com

ISBN: 0-515-12177-0

A JOVE BOOK®
Jove Books are published by The Berkley Publishing Group,
a member of Penguin Putnam Inc.,
200 Madison Avenue, New York, New York 10016.
JOVE and the "J" design are trademarks
belonging to Jove Publications, Inc.

PRINTED IN THE UNITED STATES OF AMERICA

10 9 8 7 6 5 4 3 2 1

BUSHWHACKERS

THE KILLING EDGE

1

A HEAVY, BOOMING THUNDER ROLLED OVER THE BREAKS, and gray veils of rain hung down from ominous black clouds that crowded the hills. Though it had not yet reached them, the storm was moving quickly, and Win and Joe Coulter took ponchos from their saddlebags and slipped them on to be prepared for the impending downpour.

Win was about five feet, eight inches tall, ash-blond, young in years, but with the hard face and the seasoned blue eyes of someone who had seen more than his due of hard times. Joe was six feet one with broad shoulders and darker hair. But if anyone ever doubted that he and Win were brothers, they had only to look into Joe's eyes, for they were the duplicate of Win's, and they measured life with the same reserved scrutiny.

"Win!" Joe called to his older brother. "We need to find us a place to get!"

"You think we're made of sugar, Little Brother?" Win teased. "You afraid we're goin' to melt if we get wet?"

"We won't melt, but we're goin' to be damn uncomfortable," Joe growled.

"Well, what do you say we head toward that ridge over there?" Win suggested, pointing to a long red escarpment. "Maybe we'll find an overhang to get under."

"Yeah, good idea."

The two riders broke just to the right of the trail they had been following, and the horses, perhaps anticipating the shelter of the ridge, quickened their pace without being urged to do so.

Win and Joe Coulter were in the Texas panhandle, having arrived there in a casual westward drift that neither proposed a particular destination nor had a sense of purpose. The brothers hailed from Missouri, but years of bloody border war as members of Quantrill's Raiders had set them on their wandering. They were called Bushwhackers then and still thought of themselves in such terms. Their wartime activity had earned them a degree of notoriety and, like Frank and Jesse James, the Younger brothers, and others who had ridden with them during the late war, they were now regarded as outlaws and their pictures were on reward posters in Missouri, Kansas, Arkansas, Louisiana, and even in parts of Texas.

At the end of the Civil War millions of soldiers who had worn the blue and the gray lay down their arms and picked up where they had left off. Friendships were renewed, crops were put in, men and women were married, children were born, and their lives went on as if nothing had happened.

But it was not to be so for all men. For some the wounds had cut too deeply and the price had been too dear. Families, fortunes, and dreams were consumed in flames and drowned in blood. Win and Joe were such men. They had only each other, a dwindling number of their peers, their guns, their courage, and a peculiar, though quite rigid code of honor to sustain them. For them the war had not ended. Only the battles had changed.

As they got closer to their destination they saw a small, man-made structure of rock, adobe, and wood, clinging to the base of the cliff. A wisp of smoke was curling up from the chimney.

"Look!" Joe said. "There's a cabin, and someone is in it."

"Yeah, I see it."

"Do you think whoever it is will be neighborly? It sure would be nice to dry out by a fire."

"We'll never know till we try."

They started toward the small cabin, just as the rain hit. The rain fell steadily, the big drops drumming against the ponchos, pooling, then sliding off. To the west, streaks of lightning slashed down from the dark clouds, and thunder boomed and roared. The horses, with no way to shelter themselves, occasionally shook their heads to keep the water from running into their eyes. Their manes lay wet and heavy on the sides of their necks.

When they came within hailing distance of the cabin, Win held up his hand and started to call out, but before he could do so, a puff of smoke erupted from the window, followed by the sound of a rifle shot. A singing bullet took off his hat.

"Hey! Hold on there!" Win shouted. "We don't mean you—"

The rifle fired a second time, this time hitting Joe's horse. The animal, struck in the heart, went down so quickly that Joe just barely managed to leap clear.

"Stop shooting, you son of a bitch!" Win shouted. He leaped down from his own horse, snaked the rifle from his saddle holster, then slapped the animal on the rump to get it out of the way. "Joe, you all right?" he called.

"Yeah," Joe said.

A third bullet hit the ground just beside Win, kicking up water, mud, and gravel before whining off into the valley behind him. Bending over at the waist, Win ran toward Joe, then dived for cover behind the dead horse. Joe had already done the same thing.

"What kind of fool would just open up on a couple of strangers for no reason?" Joe asked.

"I don't know," Win said. "But whoever, and whatever he is, he surely has the advantage."

"Hey in there!" Joe called. "What are you shootin' at us for? We mean you no harm!"

There was no answer.

"You reckon the son of a bitch can't speak English?" Joe asked.

"Could be," Win agreed. "Maybe he'll understand

this.'' Win fished a white handkerchief from his pocket and tied it onto the end of the rifle barrel.

"What the hell? We goin' to surrender to him?"

"Not surrendering, Little Brother," Win said. "I'm trying to get him to agree to a parley. I figure if we can get him to talk to us, we can convince him we're not his enemy.''

Win raised the white flag and began waving it back and forth. Another shot rang out from the cabin, and the bullet hit the horse not two inches away from Win.

"That does it!" Win said angrily, jacking a round into the chamber of his rifle. He rolled over onto his stomach, raised up slightly, and, resting the rifle across the body of Joe's horse, took a long, careful aim at the window. He waited and watched, and when he saw the shooter's rifle barrel come out of the window again, he aimed just to the right of it and squeezed the trigger.

The shooter in the cabin dropped his rifle, and it tumbled to the porch. An arm fell out as well and hung down motionless on the outside of the window.

"You got 'im!" Joe said.

"Yeah, I think so," Win replied. He continued to look, cautiously, toward the house. "If he was the only one."

The two brothers lay in the pouring rain for another four or five minutes, closely studying the house, which was approximately thirty-five yards away.

"He must've been the only one there," Joe finally said. "I think we should go in and get out of the rain."

"Wait," Win cautioned. "Impatience can get you killed.''

"So can pneumonia, which we're going to get if we stay out here in this rain long enough," Joe growled.

Win raised up cautiously and looked toward the house. When no one shot at him, he stood. Joe stood with him.

"Let's go in," Win said. He cocked his rifle, and the two brothers started toward the front door of the cabin.

As they approached the cabin, Win took a look around. To the left of the cabin, tucked up under the overhang of a rock, he saw two horses standing stoically in a small corral.

"There has to be two of them in there," Win said, holding up two fingers. "There are two horses."

"How come we haven't heard from the other one?" Joe asked.

"I don't know. But I think we'd better spread out a little," Win suggested. The two brothers separated themselves by several feet, while continuing their approach toward the cabin.

As they got closer to the house Win could see that the window through which their assailant had been shooting was casement style, and it was opened out, onto the porch. The shooter's arm hung down toward the porch, and Win could see that a tiny streak of blood had run down his arm and pooled onto the floor beneath his hand. When hit, the shooter had fallen against the wall just under the window.

Win approached the house from one side, Joe from the other. Signaling each other, the two brothers stepped up onto the porch, the roof of which was supported by narrow pillars. Staying close to the wall and keeping their eyes on the window in case someone else suddenly appeared, they moved cautiously toward the front door, coming from the opposite ends of the porch. Finally they reached it.

"I'll bust it open," Joe whispered. "You be ready."

Win put the rifle down and leaned it against the front wall. He pulled his pistol, pointed it toward the front door, cocked it, then looked at Joe and nodded.

Of the two brothers, Joe, though younger, was forty pounds heavier and much stronger. Using his shoulder as a battering ram, he crashed into the door. The door popped open and Joe fell to the floor, then rolled quickly to one side. Win rushed in behind him, his pistol in his hand, ready, if need be, to do battle.

No one challenged them.

Win stayed where he was for a long moment. He looked, cautiously, around the cabin, but he saw no one else. Then he went over to the window and, bending over the man who had been shooting at them, pulled him away from the wall. The shooter was a fairly small man with dirty brown hair; sun-browned, leathery skin; a hawklike nose; and a drooping moustache. There was a black hole in his forehead, the entry wound of the bullet from Win's rifle. One of the shooter's eyes was open, the other was half shut. Both had already taken on the opaque dullness of death.

"You drilled him dead center," Joe said.

"Yeah," Win agreed. He sighed as he put his pistol away. "It didn't have to be that way. Why did he shoot at us?"

Joe shrugged. "Who knows?" he asked. "Could be that he was out here alone for so long that he just plumb went loco."

"I reckon so," Win said. "Don't like killin' folks for no reason, though."

"You had a reason, Big Brother. Same reason we had for killin' men durin' the war. He was tryin' to kill us."

A very close lightning bolt, followed immediately by thunder, caused both men to jump and look toward the window. Joe laughed.

"See what I mean?" Joe said. "We just got here, and already a little thunderstorm has us jumpy."

"Yeah, well, at least we are out of the rain," Win said. He stood at the open casement window and looked out across the valley at the rain. He looked in the direction from which he and Joe had just come and realized that the shooter had enjoyed the advantage of being able to see them for several minutes before they arrived.

"Look here," Win said, pointing toward the valley. "There's no excuse for him shooting at us. He had plenty of time to watch us come up on him. He wouldn't have had to look too hard to see that we meant him no harm."

"The son of a bitch planned to kill us," Joe said. "And he would have, if he had been a better shot."

"You're right. I just don't know why he wanted to," Win agreed.

Joe looked around the cabin, then on the far side of the room he saw the source of the smoke they had seen, a small, wood-burning stove. "Hey, maybe he's got something to eat,'' he suggested. ''I'll have a look.''

Win remained by the window as his brother went over to the other side of the cabin, to the little area that served as the kitchen.

''What the hell?'' he heard Joe gasp.

Win turned quickly away from the window. ''What is it?'' he asked.

''Win, maybe you'd better get over here.''

Pulling his pistol, Win stepped quickly across the room until he was standing beside his brother. Seeing the flabbergasted expression on Joe's face, he looked in the same direction Joe was looking.

There on the floor, unnoticed by their first glance around, and looking up at them with large, frightened, deep blue eyes, was one of the most beautiful women Win had ever seen. She made no sound, because she couldn't. She was gagged, and she was bound, hands and feet.

She was also totally naked.

2

"THANK GOD!" THE WOMAN SAID AS SOON AS THE GAG was removed.

"Are you all right?" Win asked as he untied her wrists.

"No, I'm not all right," the woman answered, gasping for breath and rubbing her wrists. "You found me bound and gagged and naked. Did that seem all right to you?" The woman spoke with a very cultured accent that Win found particularly pleasing. He even appreciated the fact that her tone was more angry than whimpering.

"What I meant was, have you been . . . uh, did they harm you in any way?"

"I wasn't raped, if that's what you mean," the woman said. "And I wasn't beaten. But I have been here, in this deplorable and humiliating state, for three days. My clothes are in the corner over there. Would you please get them for me?"

"Joe," Win said. Joe, who had been standing by, unabashedly looking on, nodded then retrieved her clothes.

"You will forgive me for not playing the role of the shy maiden," the woman said. "But having been kept in this state for nearly a week and not knowing whether I was to live or die, a little thing like modesty seemed unimportant. However, now that the immediate danger has passed, perhaps you two would be so kind as to offer me your back-sides?''

''What?'' Joe asked, confused by the woman's accent and speech patterns.

The woman made a little circular motion with her hand. ''Would you turn around, please?''

''Sorry, miss,'' Win replied as he and Joe turned around. ''We had no intention of makin' you feel uncomfortable.''

''No apology necessary. You saved my life, I doubt that you could do anything now that would render me uncomfortable. Did my father send you after me?''

''No, ma'am, we don't know who your pa is. Who are you, and how did you come to be in such a predicament?''

''My father is Sir Phillip Wellington. Knowing who he is, I'm sure you can imagine what they wanted with me. I am Pamela Wellington. You may turn around now.''

''I'm afraid that still doesn't tell us too much,'' Win said.

The woman looked at them in surprise. ''You mean you've never heard of my father? Or of Camelot?''

''Camelot?''

''My father's ranch.''

Win shook his head. ''No, ma'am. My brother 'n I aren't from around here.''

''Oh, how vain I must've sounded to you just then,'' she said. Her hair was in total disarray, and she tried to push it back. Then, pulling bits of straw and lint from her hair, she examined it in her fingers. ''Oh, my God, look at this,'' she said. She looked around the room. ''I'm glad there isn't a looking glass about. If I could see how I looked now, I would really be humiliated.''

''How you look?'' Win said. He smiled. ''Well, you're a mite mussed, I'll grant you that. But I don't know as I've ever seen a prettier woman in my whole life.''

Pamela laughed. ''I'll take that as a compliment,'' she said.

''I've never heard anyone talk like you do before,'' Joe said. ''Not even a Yankee.''

''That's because I'm not a Yankee,'' Pamela said. ''I'm English.''

"You're from England? What are you doing in Texas?"

"Look, can we discuss this later?" Pamela asked. "There were four of them when I was taken. The other three rode off yesterday. I should like to be gone before they get back."

THEY WAITED ANOTHER HALF AN HOUR FOR THE STORM to pass before they left. By now Win's horse, which he had slapped on the rump to get away from the firefight, had returned and was standing quietly just outside the cabin. The two horses in the corral provided the other mounts they needed. One was the horse Pamela had been riding when she was abducted, the other had belonged to the shooter. Joe took it to replace the one the shooter had killed. Then, with Pamela pointing out the direction, they rode away, splashing through the shimmering pools of water that remained from the recent rain.

To the north, yellow and gray foothills climbed up to red buttes, guarded over by ring-tailed hawks who sailed along the walls, their sharp eyes searching for prey. To the south lay heavily timbered ridgelines, rich with the smell of sage and pine, and thickly populated by squawking blue jays and bounding deer.

Sensing that she wanted to ride in silence for a while, Win didn't ask her anything until nearly dusk. Then he asked about her father's ranch.

"It is called Camelot," Pamela answered.

"Camelot. Seems to me like I've heard that somewhere," Win said. "Wait, isn't that the name of the castle where King Arthur lived?"

"Yes, but Camelot was much more than just a castle and the town where he lived. It was a state of being, a symbol of truth and beauty," Pamela answered. "And father feels that way about Camelot. It's more than the sum total of sixty thousand acres of grasslands, purple mountains, crystal waters, two score cowboys, and thirty thousand head of cattle. It is my father's American dream, and, like King Arthur's Camelot, my father's ranch is a magical kingdom."

Joe heard none of Pamela's poetry. He heard only the hard numbers. "Sixty thousand acres?" he replied. "Damn! That's a hell of a big place." He recalled the six hundred acres his family farmed before the war. It had been considered large, for the area. He could barely imagine 60,000 acres.

"Camelot sounds like quite a place," Win said.

"It is," Pamela insisted.

They rode for the rest of the afternoon in comparative silence, then, locating a place with ample wood and a good supply of water and grass for the horses, they decided to make camp for the night.

Half an hour later they had a fire going, coffee boiling, and a freshly killed rabbit turning on a spit. Joe hobbled the horses and turned them out where they could reach water and grass.

"I hope you like rabbit," Win said. "I'm sure you are used to far grander meals."

"I'll not complain," Pamela said as she leaned back against a rock and stretched her legs out in front of her. "Though if you don't mind, I'll take water with my rabbit, rather than coffee."

"You don't drink coffee?" Win asked in surprise. "How can you not drink coffee?"

Pamela chuckled. "I'm fascinated by you Americans and your coffee. That seems to be your main staple. I much prefer tea."

"Sorry that we can't offer you any tea," Win said. "But we do have a good supply of fresh water here."

Joe, who had left camp a few minutes earlier to "have a look around," came back now to join them. "I found a spot for the lookout," he said. "We'll be high enough to have a good view in all directions, but we won't stand out against the sky."

"Good," Win said.

"Lookout?" Pamela said.

"If those other three men came back and found their friend dead today, they are already on our trail," Win said.

"Oh, I hadn't thought of that," Pamela said, putting her

hand to her mouth. "Now I've put you two in danger as well."

Win chuckled. "We've been in danger before," he said.

"I'm sure you have been," Pamela said. "Were you in the war?"

"Yes."

"The war was over before my father and I came to this country. In fact, you might say it was the war that brought us here, or rather, the depressed land prices caused by the war. But I have read about it, and I have heard others talk of it. I know that there were unspeakable horrors during the war. I assume that you and your brother fought for the Confederacy?"

"We fought with Quantrill for Missouri," Win said. "And we fought for each other. We didn't give much thought to the Confederacy, but seeing as we fought against Federal troops from the North, I guess you could say we were Rebels."

"Quantrill? I . . . I believe I have heard of him."

"What have you heard?"

"That he was a murderer and despoiler of women and children," Pamela said. "Surely, you and your brother didn't ally yourselves with such a man?"

"Ally ourselves with such a man?" Win replied. He shook his head. "Don't you understand, Miss Wellington? We *are* such men."

"But surely you are not, sir. Otherwise, you wouldn't have rescued me." Suddenly she gasped, as if coming to a realization. "Unless you *haven't* rescued me, but have merely replaced my captors. Is that the case?"

Neither Win nor Joe answered her question, and she looked at them anxiously as Joe tested the rabbit with his knife, declared it done, then cut it into serving sizes and lay it out on a flat rock. He opened a little pouch of salt and sprinkled it on the meat, then stepped back.

Though she was hungry, Pamela held back until she was invited.

"Thank you," she mumbled, taking a piece of the meat then sitting back down, keeping a wary eye on her two rescuers . . . if indeed that was what they were.

"I'll take the first watch," Joe said, taking some of the meat and a cup of coffee with him.

Win unrolled his bedroll beside a rock, then looked over at Pamela.

"You can sleep here," he said. "I'll use Joe's blankets. We won't be sleeping at the same time, anyway."

"You haven't answered my question," Pamela said.

"What question?"

"Have you become my captors?"

"Is that what you think?"

"I . . . I don't know what to think. By your own admission you and your brother rode for Quantrill."

"And that means what? That we don't quite come up to your image of Knights of the Round Table, rescuing fair damsels from dragons?" Win said.

"You might say that," Pamela admitted, surprised by Win's reference.

Win sighed. "We are not your captors, Miss Wellington," he said. He pointed toward the darkness. "You are free to go now, if you wish."

"No," Pamela said. "I'm sorry I questioned you. I would prefer to stay, if you don't mind."

"You can stay," Win said.

Pamela smiled. "Thank you," she said. "And I'm sorry I questioned you."

"That's all right," Win said. "But I suggest you get some sleep now."

"Good idea," Pamela said, pulling the blanket over her shoulders and closing her eyes.

Win laid out Joe's blanket as well, then, taking off his boots and unbuckling his gun belt, he crawled into the bed.

IT SEEMED LIKE ONLY MOMENTS LATER THAT JOE WAS shaking him gently.

"Time already? All right, I'm getting up," Win said, reaching for his boots.

"It's not that," Joe hissed. "We've got company comin'."

Win was instantly awake. "How far?" he asked.

" 'Bout a mile back down the trail," Joe said. "I seen 'em first when one of 'em lit up a pipe. And the moon is shinin' so bright that I was able to see 'em again when they forded the river. There's three of 'em."

"If there are three, then it must be them," Pamela said, having been awakened by Joe and Win's whispering. Her voice was touched with fear.

"You want to saddle up and ride on?" Joe asked.

Win stroked his chin for a minute and thought, then he shook his head.

"No," he said. "Let's make 'em do what we want them to do. Throw some more wood on the campfire. Let's get it going well."

"The campfire? But won't that lead them right to us?" Pamela asked.

"That's what I'm counting on," Win replied.

When the campfire was built up, Win and Joe brought in some pine boughs to cover with the blankets, thus providing silhouettes for the bedrolls. Then, quietly, Win, Joe, and Pamela moved about twenty yards to the west, behind a rock outcropping. There, they waited.

Pamela was with Win, Joe was about fifteen yards south of them. The three men trailing would be approaching from the east.

Pamela reached over to put her hand on him. It was a move designed to calm her own fears; she just needed to know that she wasn't here alone. In the dark, however, her hand moved across his upper thigh, then lay on the front of his pants. Feeling it there, and remembering the sight of her nude, Win experienced an immediate erection. Until that moment, Pamela had thought that her hand was resting innocently on his leg. When she felt his sudden, surging reaction, however, she realized where her hand was, and what she had done. She gasped, and quickly moved it away.

"I'm sorry, I'm sorry!" she apologized in the dark.

"Under the circumstances, so am I," Win said with a little chuckle. Then, hearing something, he added, "Shhh!"

They sat there very quietly, with Win's gaze sweeping

back and forth, looking for any movement in the dark. He had learned long ago that his night vision worked better by not looking directly at an object, but by looking off to one side. He didn't know why that was, but it was a technique that he had used frequently and he was using it now.

From somewhere out in the darkness a small pebble was dislodged. Win felt, rather than heard, Pamela stiffen beside him, and he knew that she had heard it too. He reached over to touch her reassuringly, and also as a caution to remain quiet.

According to the position of the stars, Win knew that it was now about midnight. If Joe hadn't awakened him earlier, he would have been awakening him now anyway.

Win remained very still and looked around slowly, still not concentrating on any one spot. Using this sweeping technique, he detected movement, silent shadows slipping through the darkness. He saw two, then the third.

The three men moved on into the camp where they stood, guns drawn, in the glow of the fire. One of them, obviously the leader of the three, held up his finger to get the attention of the other two. He pointed to the sleeping rolls where Win and Joe had put their boots. It was obviously their intention to kill whoever had come for Pamela, then take her back with them. The three men pointed their guns at the two sleeping rolls.

"Now!" the leader of the three shouted, and he fired first. The other two fired immediately afterward, the muzzle flashes of their pistols lighting up the night.

Win stood up and fired, using the twelve-inch wide muzzle blast of one of the shooters as his target. When he opened up, Joe did as well. All three assailants were hit in the opening fusillade, and though they tried to return fire, their efforts had no more effect than to add to the pulses of light that were now emanating from Win's and Joe's guns.

Had anyone within a distance of several miles been witness to the event, they would have reported a series of lightning flashes, for indeed, that's what they were. The trees and rocks were illuminated in bursts of stark white and featureless black, and Pamela watched with horrid fascination as the three assailants' faces contorted in pain and shock.

The shooting stopped, though the sounds of the last reports continued to echo back from the steep side of a distant mesa. Finally even the echoes played out, and absolute silence returned.

"Joe," Win called out to his brother. When he didn't get an answer he called again, with a bit more urgency. "Joe? You all right?"

"Yeah," Joe answered, his voice right on top of them now, for he had walked back to join Win and Pamela. "I'm all right. How about you two?"

"We're fine," Win said. He looked over at Pamela, who, though uninjured, was still in a state of semi-shock. "Did you get a look at them?" he asked.

Pamela nodded, but she said nothing.

"Are they the same ones who took you?"

"I think so. I didn't get that good a look at them."

"How about taking a good look now?"

Pamela shivered. "Do I have to?"

"I know it won't be pleasant," Win said. "But we need to know if these are the same ones. If one of them is different, that means there could still be someone out there after you."

Pamela nodded, then she stuck her hand out toward Win, asking silently that he take hold of it. He did, and leading her gently through the rocks, they walked to look down upon the three corpses. Two were already on their backs, the third was facedown. Win turned him over with his boot. Squeezing Win's hand, Pamela studied the faces.

"Yes," she finally said. "That's all of them."

"What do we do with them now?" Joe asked.

"Leave them," Win said. "We'll move our camp about a mile on down the road."

"Thanks," Pamela said. "I wasn't looking forward to spending another night with them around . . . even if they are dead."

3

NEITHER WIN NOR JOE HAD EVER SEEN ANYTHING LIKE IT back in Missouri. The house was huge, with cupolas, and dormers, and so many windows that the morning sun flashed back in such brilliance that it almost looked as if the house were on fire.

The house reminded Win of a wedding cake he had once seen, white and tiered. And not just the house. Even the surrounding lawn was built up in a series of terraces, which worked up from the road to the base of the house itself. A large, white-graveled driveway made a U in front of the house where a coach and four sat at the ready, its highly polished paint job glistening in the morning sun. A crest of some sort was on the door of the coach.

Win and Joe stopped at an intricately carved oak hitching rail, then slid down from their saddles and tied off their horses. Win helped Pamela down.

As they started toward the broad steps leading up to the front porch, the front door suddenly opened, and two men came out, carrying rifles. The rifles were pointed at Joe and Win.

"Put your hands up and let my daughter go!" one of the men shouted, staring down the barrel of his rifle.

"Father, no!" Pamela shouted quickly. "These gentlemen aren't my abductors! They are my rescuers!"

The man who had challenged them, a tall, broad-shouldered man with a full head of snow-white hair, raised his head and allowed the end of his rifle to lower.

"What's that? Your rescuers, you say?"

"Yes, Father. They found me and brought me back safely."

"Bascomb, lower your piece," the man ordered, setting his own rifle down and leaning it against the front wall of the house.

"Very good, sir," Bascomb replied. Bascomb was wearing a starched shirt, with paper collar, tie, and a cutaway jacket. Pamela's father was wearing denim trousers and a plain white shirt. Smiling, he came down the steps with his arms spread wide, smothering his daughter in a bearlike embrace.

"Thank God you have been safely returned to me," he said. "I have nearly every hand out looking for you, and I've notified the sheriffs in three counties. I posted a reward—" He stopped in mid-sentence and looked at Win and Joe. "The reward, I nearly forgot. But, of course, that is yours now."

"Mr. Wellington, we didn't bring her back for a reward," Win said. "We didn't even know about it."

"You didn't know about it? How could you not know? I put the word out everywhere."

"We just rode into this part of the country," Win said.

"Father, they didn't know who I was when they found me. And they had never even heard of you."

"Never heard of me? My word," Wellington said. "Well, that is certainly bruising to one's ego."

Pamela laughed. "A little ego deflation is good for you," she said. "Otherwise, it might get so big that the entire state of Texas couldn't hold it."

"Yes, well, it doesn't matter," Wellington said. "The important thing is you have been brought home, none the worse for wear." Suddenly he stopped and stared intensely at her for a long moment. "You *are* none the worse for wear, aren't you, my dear? I mean . . . uh, you weren't . . ."
He let the question hang, unfinished.

"I'm fine, Father," Pamela said quickly. "I wasn't raped."

Wellington cleared his throat in embarrassment. "That doesn't change anything. As soon as those blackguards are found, I shall see to it that they are brought to justice."

"It's a little late for that," Win said.

"Late? What do you mean? It's never too late."

"What he means, Father, is that the four men who did this have already been brought to justice."

"They're in jail?" Wellington asked.

"They're dead," Win said.

"Dead?"

"My brother and I killed them."

"My word," Wellington said. "You two men don't pussyfoot around, do you?"

"Pussyfoot around?" Win repeated. He laughed. "No, I reckon you might say we don't do that."

"Where are my manners?" Wellington asked. He extended his hand. "My name is Wellington, Phillip J. Wellington. And you two are . . . ?"

"I'm Win Coulter. This is my brother, Joe," Win said, shaking Wellington's hand. Joe shook it next.

"Well, Mr. Win and Joe Coulter, it doesn't matter whether you knew about the reward or not, it is yours to claim, nevertheless," Wellington said. "I offered five thousand dollars to whoever would bring my daughter back to me, unharmed, and you two have done so. Therefore, the money is yours. That is, unless you have some aversion to money."

"No, Mr. Wellington, we don't have an aversion to money," Win said.

"Ah, good, then you'll take it," Wellington said. "If you'll wait right here, I'll get it for you."

"Father, we can do more than that," Pamela said, stopping her father as he started back up the steps. Wellington looked over at her.

"You have something else in mind?" he asked.

Pamela smiled up at Win. "I thought you might at least invite them to have lunch with us," she suggested.

"Yes, of course," Wellington replied quickly. "I would, indeed, be honored if you would stay for lunch." He pointed toward the bunkhouse. "You can clean up in there, if you'd like."

Win chuckled. "Mr. Wellington, we accept your invitation, but you've never seen my brother eat. He can put a serious dint in your supplies."

Wellington laughed heartily. "Not to worry, my boy," he said. "We're having beef, and since there are more than thirty thousand of the creatures on the place, I expect there'll be enough." He pointed to the barn. "You can unsaddle your horses and turn them loose in there until you are ready for them again. They'll find plenty of food and water."

"Thanks," Win said.

An hour later Win and Joe returned to the main house. They had washed at the pump on the porch of the bunkhouse and put on the clean shirts they had in their saddlebags. Their other shirts were almost immediately taken from them by a Mexican laundress, and were now clean and hanging from a clothesline to dry.

They were met at the front door by the man who had stood alongside Wellington when he accosted them at rifle point earlier.

"You're Bunkem?" Win asked.

"Bascomb, sir," the man corrected. He too had an accent.

"You're English too, aren't you?" Joe asked.

"Yes, sir."

"Are you kin?"

"I beg your pardon, sir?"

"You part of the family?"

"Oh, heavens no, sir. I'm in the service."

"The service?"

"It's like being part of the family," Pamela said, arriving at that moment. "Mr. Bascomb has worked for my father for many years, and Mr. Bascomb's father worked for my grandfather. In fact, the relationship goes back for four generations. Men who hold such positions refer to themselves as being 'in the service,' and it is a very old and very honorable profession.''

When Win saw Pamela, he couldn't hold back the gasp of surprise. He would be hard-pressed to identify this as the same young woman he first saw yesterday. That woman had been a naked waif, a poor, bedraggled creature who was only barely managing to cling to humanity.

The woman who greeted them now looked as if she had stepped down from a fine oil painting. She was wearing an off-the-shoulder dress with a neckline that plunged low enough to show the top of her breasts, though a red silk rose, strategically placed at the cleavage, helped preserve some modesty. The dress itself was clinging, yellow silk, overlaid with lace. Her coiffure featured a pile of curls on top, and a French roll which hung down her neck. A gold chain was around her neck, and from the chain dangled a large pearl.

Win had never seen anyone quite like this before. It was as if he were being confronted by a queen or a princess come to life.

Pamela grew uneasy with the expressions on the faces of Win and Joe, and, with a nervous laugh, she touched her hair.

''Have I gone green?'' she asked.

''What?''

''You are both staring with such intensity,'' she said.

''Oh, I'm . . . I'm sorry,'' Win apologized. ''It's just that you look so . . . I mean, I've never seen . . .'' He paused, then continued, changing his line of thought. ''Uh, that is, I had no idea lunch would be such a dressy affair. I'm afraid these shirts are all we have.''

''If you wish, madam, I believe I could find some jackets for them,'' Bascomb suggested. ''Though, for the larger gentleman, it might be quite ill-fitting.''

''Never mind, Mr. Bascomb, they are fine just as they are,'' Pamela said.

''To be sure,'' Bascomb said, looking at the two brothers with ill-concealed disapproval. ''This way, gentlemen.''

''That's all right, Mr. Bascomb, I'll take them to the

dining room," Pamela said. Smiling at the two brothers, she stepped between them and offered each of them an arm.

They walked down a long, wide hall, with a floor that was so highly polished it reflected the items of furniture standing on it as clearly as if it were a mirror. Along the way, as if standing guard, were several polished suits of armor and painted shields. All the shields were decorated with the same crest. Against a white background, a blue mailed fist clutched a golden sword, placed at the intersection of a red St. Andrew's cross.

"That's the same thing that's on the door of the coach," Joe said, pointing to one of the shields.

"That's the coat of arms of the Earldom of Dunliegh," Pamela said. "I am told, by the way, that a distant ancestor of mine, the first Earl of Dunliegh, wore this very suit of armor in the Battle of Agincourt," she added, pointing to one of the iron suits.

"Ha! Joe, I'd hate to see you try and get into something like that," Win said. "You wouldn't even be able to get your arm inside it."

"Was this here fella a full-grown man at the time?" Joe asked.

Pamela laughed. "Oh, yes. But the Battle of Agincourt happened over four hundred years ago, and I believe people were smaller then."

"Four hundred years?" Win gasped. "You can keep track of your kin that long?"

"That is an important date in our family, for that was when Geoffrey Wellington was invested with the Earldom of Dunliegh," Pamela explained.

"What is this earldom?" Joe asked.

"English peers come in several degrees of importance," Pamela explained. "At the top of the order are dukes, followed by marquesses, then earls, then viscounts, then barons. My father is . . . or was, an earl."

"Pamela, all that is of no concern here," Phillip Wellington said, meeting them in the doorway of the dining room at that moment. "I'm sure our guests are not interested in our quaint customs."

Wellington was wearing a white uniform of some sort, with a red sash running diagonally across his chest, gold-fringed epaulets on his shoulders, and a splash of medals on his breast.

"I think it's very interesting," Win said. "I've read about kings and lords and knights and so forth, but I've never met anyone like that before now."

"Yes, well, technically, dear boy, you haven't met one now," Wellington said. "As Pamela told you, it was necessary for me to give up the title, and my land, when I left England to come to the United States."

"Did it bother you to give it up?"

"Not at all. I firmly believe that your founding fathers were quite right to dispense with titles. They are oppressive to the common man and burdensome to the peerage. But enough of that. If you'll come this way, gentlemen, I believe lunch is ready."

Wellington led them into the dining room. The dining room was a very large room with polished oak wainscoting running halfway up the walls, and flocked cream and green wallpaper finishing it off. At strategic spots around the room large portraits hung by wires from the picture rail. One of the portraits was of Phillip Wellington astride a horse, wearing the same uniform he was wearing now. Another was of a beautiful woman. For a moment, Win thought it was a portrait of Pamela. Upon a closer examination, however, he realized that the young girl standing beside the woman *was* Pamela.

"That was my mother," Pamela said, noticing where Win was looking. "She died the year before we left England."

"She was very beautiful."

"Yes, she was," Wellington agreed.

"I see that you are wearing the same sort of clothes in that painting that you are now," Win said. "Is that a military uniform of some kind?"

"Yes," Wellington said. "I still hold a brigadier's commission in the Royal Reserves, though I seriously doubt that the Queen will ever call me to active duty."

"My father fought in the Crimean War," Pamela said. "He was at Balaclava as a lieutenant in the Light Brigade. You may have heard of the famous poem written by Tennyson: 'Theirs not to make reply, Theirs not to reason why . . . ' "

" 'Theirs but to do and die,' " Win continued, taking over the poem. " 'Into the Valley of Death rode the six hundred.' Yes, I have heard of it."

"I'm very impressed," Pamela said.

"I was always impressed by the bravery of those soldiers," Win said. "It's an honor to actually meet one of them."

"I was young and imprudent. It was a foolish battle in a war fought with honor but no sense," Wellington said. "Of the six hundred troops we committed to the charge, four hundred were killed. But then, I needn't tell you gentlemen such things. Your country, and my daughter tells me that you, personally, have come through your own war with battles just as foolish, and just as deadly. Suppose we change the subject?"

Wellington pointed to the center of the dining room where there was a very long table, covered with a damask tablecloth and set with crystal candelabra, silver chargers, and glistening china. "Won't you be seated?" he invited.

The meal was brought to the table in various courses. Win didn't think he had ever tasted anything as good, and Joe obviously concurred, for his appetite and acceptance of "seconds" was so prodigious that, before the end of the meal, a few of the kitchen staff sneaked unobtrusively to the door to get a look at the man who could eat so much.

After the meal Wellington invited Win and Joe into his library. Here, twenty-foot-tall bookshelves lined the walls, and books filled the shelves. Wellington gestured toward a cluster of leather chairs, and they all sat down. There, Wellington gave them the reward he had promised. In addition, brandy was served and Pamela offered them cigars. When the offer was accepted, she trimmed the ends and ran her tongue down the length of each side. Then she lit each of them.

"Gentlemen, if you think I am plying you with food, drink, and tobacco for a specific reason, you are right," Wellington said. "I want you in a good mood when I attempt to make my case."

"Make your case?" Joe asked. He took the cigar out of his mouth and examined the burning tip. He had never had one this good. "What case is that?"

"I want you two men to come to work for me."

Win shook his head no. "We appreciate the job offer, Mr. Wellington," he said. "We really do. But I'm afraid you wouldn't be getting your money's worth out of us. Neither one of us are cowhands."

Wellington studied them for a moment over the rim of his brandy snifter.

"Who said anything about making you into cowhands?" he asked.

Win looked confused. "Then I don't understand. If you don't intend to make us into cowhands, what do you want with us?"

"I want to hire you for the skill you have already demonstrated. When you killed those men who took my daughter, you proved yourselves to be quite skilled with your weapons."

"You want to hire our guns, you mean?" Win replied.

"In a manner of speaking, yes."

Win shook his head. "We aren't hired killers."

"Are you trying to tell me you have scruples, Mr. Coulter? Scruples from men who rode with Quantrill?"

Win stood up quickly, and when he did so, Joe stood up as well.

"Mr. Wellington, I thank you for the great meal, the good brandy, and the fine cigars. But I think my brother and I will be going on now."

"No, wait . . . please . . . wait," Wellington called, holding out his hand. He paused for a moment, pinching the bridge of his nose as if trying to gather his thoughts. "I'm sorry, the remark about a lack of scruples was quite boorish, and I beg your forgiveness. It's just that I find myself in a country that is rough and unforgiving, a country for which my experience has left me totally unprepared. Witness the scheme to abduct my daughter for ransom. If you two had not happened along at the right moment, it might have resulted in an unthinkable disaster. Luckily, you spoiled their scheme.''

"We spoiled their scheme all right,'' Win said. "In fact, you might say we spoiled it permanently.''

Wellington waved his hand. "I know, I know, you killed them all, and good riddance. I wish I could say that with their demise all danger had passed, but in the atmosphere of lawlessness that prevails, who is to say some others won't conceive of the same plan? And, of course, there are also rustlers to contend with. You said that you were not hired killers, Mr. Coulter. Well, that is good, for I have no wish to employ killers. I do, however, want to hire people who might be able to provide a measure of safety for my daughter and me, and might, at the same time, deter the lawless elements from their adventures.''

"Aren't you afraid that you might be jumping from the frying pan into the fire?'' Win asked.

"Are you suggesting that I might be putting myself in danger by hiring you?'' Wellington asked.

"You are in no danger from us, Mr. Wellington. But you were right when you accused us of riding for Quantrill. As bushwhackers, we did a lot of robbing, burning, and killing. We aren't choirboys, Mr. Wellington. We're outlaws, wanted in several states. Are you so willing to hire outlaws?''

"I am willing to hire men of honor,'' Wellington said. "And though you claim to be outlaws, and I've no reason to dispute that claim, you have also proven to me that you are men of honor.''

"Please, Win, Joe,'' Pamela said. "I know, after all you have done for me, that I have no right to ask for anything more . . . but we need you.''

"You have five thousand dollars coming as a reward for rescuing my daughter. I will double that, if you'll stay for one month,'' Wellington said.

"Five thousand dollars for one month's work?'' Joe

asked. He whistled. "Lord almighty, that kind of pay could make an honest man of me! Win, I say we stay. And if you don't want to, I'll stay by myself."

Win sighed, then chuckled. "All right, we'll stay."

4

IN THE NEARBY TOWN OF LORAINE, PEOPLE WERE GOING about their business on the main street when a stranger rode in. He pulled up near the Black Horse Saloon, dismounted, and tied his horse to the hitch rail. The townspeople watched him with increasing curiosity as he took off his hat and rubbed a handkerchief across his face. His hair and eyebrows were snow-white, and his skin was as pale as any skin they had ever seen. He glanced toward them with eyes that had a light pinkish tinge but were otherwise as colorless as glass.

The albino was wearing a gun strapped low on his right hip. He looked up and down the street, then, not appearing to take notice of two men who were standing on the porch of the building next door to the Black Horse, he went inside.

"You know who that is?" one of the men asked after the albino was through the swinging doors and out of hearing.

"I ain't never seen him before," the other answered. "But I've heard him described. That's gotta be—"

"Lucas Shardeen," the first one interrupted, as though he didn't want to be cheated out of saying it. "They say he's faster'n greased lightnin' with that gun of his. They say he's gunned down more'n ten men in fair fights."

"I was goin' to say that," the other replied. "I know'd who it was the moment I seen him. I didn't need you to tell me."

"Well, I'll just bet you don't know what he's doin' here," the first one said.

"No, I don't. But if he's lookin' for anyone, I sure wouldn't want to be that person."

"He's come to work for Chad Emmerline, out at the Double-Diamond."

"That feller's come to work at the Double-Diamond? Ha! He sure don't seem like no cowpuncher to me."

"I don't figure he's goin' to be punchin' any cows."

"Then what is he goin' to be doin'?"

"If you ask me, he'll be doin' what he's been doin'. Killin'," the first answered matter-of-factly.

Inside the saloon, Shardeen stepped up to the bar, and the bartender hurried over to see what he wanted. At the opposite end of the bar a couple of cowboys flanked a young woman. They were talking and laughing, and pouring drinks from the bottle of whiskey that sat in front of them.

"Whiskey," Shardeen ordered.

"Yes, sir, Mr. Shardeen," the bartender answered nervously. He took a glass from under the counter and, with shaking hands, poured Shardeen a drink.

"You know where the Double-Diamond is?" Shardeen asked.

"Yes, sir, I do. It's about five miles northwest of here," the bartender replied.

"Hey, mister," one of the two cowboys at the end of the bar called. "You goin' to work on the Double-Diamond?"

Shardeen looked toward the cowboy, but he didn't answer.

"The reason I ask is, me an' ole Snake here, we punch cows for Clyde Carter. He owns the Cripple C, right next to the Double-Diamond. That makes us neighbors. Ain't that right, Snake?"

"That's right, Dooley," Snake answered.

Snake and Dooley were both in their mid-twenties. They were typical-looking working cowboys, wearing their prized Stetsons, vests, and leather chaps. Both were wearing pistols, though the guns were worn high and strapped in for ease of riding and working.

"You goin' to be cookin' for Emmerline?" Dooley asked. "Reason I asked is, you don't much look like a cowboy, if you'll excuse me for sayin' so."

Shardeen raised his glass to his thin, colorless lips and stared at Dooley, Snake, and the woman with them through pink eyes, set in an expressionless face. He said nothing.

"Course . . . they ain't nothin' wrong with bein' a cook," Dooley went on. Shardeen's cold, expressionless stare was beginning to make him nervous.

"Honey, quit talkin' to him," the woman whispered. "He scares me."

"Now, how can that little fella scare you?" Dooley replied. "Hell, look at him. Skinned and gutted, he wouldn't dress out any more'n one 'fifteen, maybe one 'twenty pounds."

Shardeen turned back toward the bar. "I want a woman," he said to the bartender.

"I, uh, am sorry, sir," the bartender replied. "But we have no women available."

"I'll take that one," Shardeen said, pointing to the woman with the two cowboys.

"It is my belief that the two young men with her have engaged her for the entire afternoon."

"They ain't doin' nothin' but talkin' to her," Shardeen said.

"Yes, sir, but once they pay their money, it is their prerogative how they spend their time."

"You," Shardeen said to the woman. "Come on, we're goin' upstairs."

"What?" the woman replied.

"You heard me. I said we're goin' upstairs."

"Mister, maybe you didn't notice," Dooley said. "But Lucy is with my pard and me."

"You ain't doin' nothin' but talkin' to her," Shardeen

said. "When I'm finished with her, I'll send her back down."

Dooley looked at the bartender. "Tell you what," he said. "Our pale-skinned friend there is new here, so maybe he don't understand the word 'manners.' That bein' the case, I won't go down there and kick the shit out of 'im."

"Dooley, no!" the bartender hissed, sliding down the bar quickly toward him. "Don't you know who that is?"

"No."

"His name is Shardeen. Lucas Shardeen," the bartender said, as if the name would explain everything.

"Still don't mean nothin' to me," Dooley said. "Except that he looks like a maggot that crawled out from under a rotten log."

"Please!" the bartender hissed. "Don't make him mad."

"Don't make him mad? Why don't you tell that little pissant not to make *me* mad?"

"Dooley, I don't have a good feelin' about this," Snake whispered. Then, more loudly, to the bartender he added, "Bartender, why don't you pour our new neighbor another drink, on us?"

"Yes, I'll be happy to," the bartender said, smiling broadly in an attempt to defuse the situation.

"I don't want another drink. I want the woman," Shardeen said. He started down toward them and raised his hand. Dooley stepped in front of him.

"Mister, I've had about as much as I'm goin' to take from you. You touch that woman and I'm goin' to knock you on your ass," he said menacingly.

Shardeen grunted with contempt, stepped around the cowboy's outstretched hand, and put his hand on Lucy's shoulder. Lucy whimpered in fear, and before Shardeen's hand closed, Dooley hit him.

Shardeen's reputation as a killer had, long ago, precluded even the biggest men from actually challenging him. As a result, he was taken completely by surprise, and he caught the punch on his jaw, then went to the floor like a sack of potatoes.

Dooley laughed. "I told you what I was goin' to do,"

he said apologetically. He reached down to help Shardeen up. "Now, why don't you just leave us and the woman alone? Drink the drink my pard and I bought you, and forget it."

Shardeen smoothed his clothes, then glared at Dooley.

"Pull your gun, mister," he said.

"What?"

"I said, pull your gun. Or give me the woman."

"The woman ain't goin' with you."

"Dooley," Lucy said in a frightened voice. "Dooley, I'll go with him. It ain't worth gettin' killed for."

"Hell no, you ain't goin' with him," Dooley said. "Mister, the bartender here tells me your name is Shardeen, like that's s'posed to mean somethin' to me. Well, let me tell you somethin', it don't mean shit to me. Now, if you're wantin' to put up your fists and fight like a man, I aim to oblige you."

"Don't be a fool, Dooley," the bartender said. "Shardeen may be the fastest man with a gun there ever was."

"Fast with a gun? That don't mean nothin' to me," Dooley said. "I ain't plannin' on fightin' him with a gun." He doubled up his fist. "All I aim to do is bruise the little shit up some."

"I'm goin' to kill you, cowboy," Shardeen said, his voice cold, flat, and totally without expression.

"Told you, I ain't goin' to get in no gunfight with you," Dooley said.

"Come on, Dooley," Snake said. "This here is makin' me nervous. Let's get on back to the ranch."

"And leave this pretty girl here, all alone?"

"Go on, Dooley," Lucy said, her voice rising in panic. "I mean it. I ain't goin' to stay with you."

Dooley looked at Shardeen again, then he sighed. "All right, mister, this is your lucky day," he finally said. "Looks like I ain't goin' to beat the shit out of you after all. Come on, Snake, let's go. I reckon we can come back when the company's a little better."

"You won't reach your horse alive," Shardeen warned.

"Why not? You goin' to shoot me in the back?"

"Could be."

"To hell with you, mister," Dooley said. "Come on, Snake, let's go."

Dooley and Snake started toward the door. The two men who had watched Shardeen arrive, and who had been peering over the batwing doors from outside to see what was going on, now stepped to one side to let Dooley and Snake come through. The albino followed them.

"You ain't goin' nowhere, mister," Shardeen said.

On the porch now, Dooley turned to face Shardeen. In addition to the two men who were already there, a few others, made curious by the scene being played out on the boardwalk in front of the Black Horse, began drifting over to watch.

"I'm riding out of here," Dooley said again. The gravity of his situation had finally sunk in, and the bravado was gone . . . replaced by a nervous tick in his voice.

"I'll make it easy on you," Shardeen said. "I'm going to count to three. You can pull your gun any time you want, but you'd better do it before I get to three 'cause that's when I'm pulling mine."

"I . . . I don't want to do this," Dooley said. Now his voice reflected naked fear.

"You ain't got no choice," Shardeen said. "One . . ."

"Snake?" Dooley called.

"You . . . you goin' to take us both on, mister?" Snake asked, holding his hand out over his pistol.

"Two."

Dooley made a desperate grab for his pistol. Shardeen smiled at him and waited for Dooley to clear leather before he started for his own gun. Snake hesitated a second, then he began his draw as well.

For just a moment, Dooley and Snake had the irrational idea that they might just win, and wild smiles began to spread across their faces. Then Shardeen's shoulder jumped and a pistol appeared in his hand, already blazing. The first shot caught Dooley in the chest, and he stumbled back off the porch, pulling the trigger of his own gun as he did so, sending a slug into the boards. Shardeen's second shot hit

Snake between the eyes, and he fell backward, his arms flopped out uselessly beside him. He didn't even get off a shot.

"My God! Did you see that?"

"He didn't even start to draw till them two boys already had their guns out 'n still he beat 'em!"

"Sweet Jesus, I ain't never seen nothin' like that!"

Shardeen stood there for a moment, the gun still smoking in his hand as he looked down at the bodies of the two men he had just killed. Then he looked out at the men who had gathered to watch.

"Anyone here thinkin' maybe this wasn't a fair fight?" Shardeen asked.

"Not me," someone replied.

"They drew first," another said.

"It was a fair fight. Yes, sir, fair and square," another voice added.

"Good," Shardeen said, holstering his gun. "Thought you might see it my way."

Several in the crowd walked over to get a closer look at the two dead cowboys. Dooley's feet, covered by well-worn boots, were turned out at an unusual angle. Snake's feet, covered with the fine snakeskin boots that gave him his nickname, were pointing straight up. Snake's eyes were still open. Dooley's eyes were shut.

"Get 'em out of here," the bartender growled. "Can't leave them out like that. It's bad for business."

"What do you want to do with 'em?"

"Drag 'em over to the corner of the building there and cover 'em with a tarp till the undertaker gets here," the bartender suggested.

Shardeen, with an indifferent shrug, pushed his way back through the batwing doors. Lucy was cowering in the corner of the saloon.

"You . . . you killed those men," she said.

"No, I didn't. You killed them," Shardeen replied.

"What do you mean, I killed them?"

"You shoulda gone upstairs with me when I asked you

the first time. Now, see how foolish it was for you to say no to me? Your friends are both dead, and you are going upstairs with me, just like I wanted. Kind of funny when you think about it, ain't it?'' he added, laughing cruelly.

5

AT CAMELOT, APPROXIMATELY TEN MILES DISTANT FROM Loraine and Lucas Shardeen, Win and Joe Coulter were just outside the bunkhouse when nearly a dozen men rode in. The cowboys were tired and worn-looking, as if they had ridden long and hard. They rode straight to the watering troughs, dismounted, and began removing their saddles as the horses drank thirstily. Some of the men stuck their heads down into the same troughs, or filled their hats which they then put on, letting the water cascade down across their faces.

At first the cowboys were shouting and laughing back and forth to each other in such an animated and self-contained way that no one noticed Win and Joe. In fact, the first sign anyone had that there were strangers in their midst was when someone saw Pamela's horse in the corral.

"Hey, lookie there!" one of the cowboys said as he turned his own mount loose. "Ain't that the horse Miss Wellington was ridin' when she was took?"

"I believe it was," one of the others said. "She must be back."

"Unless the horse come back on its own."

"The horse didn't come back on his own. Miss Wellington is back," Win said as he and Joe walked out to join the men who had just returned.

Surprised to see a couple of strangers amidst them, the cowboys turned toward them in curiosity. Then the one who appeared to be the leader came over to meet them. He was a short, bandy-legged man with a scar on his cheek that looked like a purple lightning flash.

"The name is Brown, Edward Brown, though most folks just call me Cherokee," he said. "How do you know Miss Wellington is back?"

"Because my brother and I brought her back," Win said.

"You the sons of bitches that took her?" one of the other cowboys asked menacingly.

"Easy, Pete, easy," Cherokee said, holding out his hand. "If they're the ones that took her, I don't think they'd be hanging around here right now."

"You're a smart man," Win said.

Cherokee smiled, though the scar on his cheek had obviously severed the muscles on one side of his mouth because the smile pulled his lips out of shape. "Yeah, well, maybe that's why Mr. Wellington made me the foreman," he said. "We been lookin' ever'where for Miss Wellington. The boss must've been real pleased to see you two boys bring her in. Are you looking for work?"

"We already have work," Win said.

"Mr. Wellington hired us," Joe explained easily.

"Is that a fact?" Cherokee asked. He lay his finger alongside his scar and rubbed it thoughtfully for a moment.

"That's right," Win said.

"All right, what's done is done, I reckon," he finally said. He pointed a short, crooked finger at Win and Joe. "But just so's you understand . . . I am the ramrod around this here outfit. Mr. Wellington mighta hired you, but you'll be takin' your orders from me, just like all the other cattle hands."

"We're not cattle hands," Win said.

Cherokee looked surprised. "What do you mean, you ain't cattle hands? If you ain't, what the hell did Wellington hire you for? What do you plan on doin'?"

"Whatever Mr. Wellington wants us to do," Win answered easily.

Cherokee's eyes narrowed. It was obvious that he didn't particularly like the setup, but it was also obvious that there was nothing he could do about it.

"All right," he finally said with a snarl. "If Mr. Wellington wants to hire you, that's his business. Maybe it's his way of rewardin' you for findin' his daughter. But if you two ain't workin' for me, then you stay the hell out of my way, do you hear me? I got no time for you. Where are you bunkin' down?"

"What's wrong with the bunkhouse?" Win asked.

"The bunkhouse is for cowboys. Workin' cowboys," Cherokee added. "There's a place behind the tack room. You two can bunk in there."

"Sounds good enough to us," Win said.

"Long as there's a place at the table for us," Joe added. He took a step closer to Cherokee and looked down on him. "And I intend to see to it that there is," he added menacingly.

"Sure, there won't be no problem with you boys settin' at the table," Cherokee said.

JOE WAS OUT JUST AFTER BREAKFAST THE NEXT MORNING. He enjoyed working with his hands, so when he saw that the wheels of one of the wagons needed to be packed with grease, he didn't ask anyone about it. Instead, he merely went about getting the blocks in place and the wheels off, then he started packing the hubs by hand.

Win was about to help him when Wellington came out to talk to them.

"You don't have to do that kind of work," Wellington said.

"I know I don't have to," Joe said, standing up and touching the back of his hand to his forehead. He left a small smear of grease. "But it reminds me of another time . . . another place. I like it."

"Then, by all means, don't let me stop you," Wellington said. Then he looked over at Win. "Win, I would appreciate it if you would come riding with me this morning. I just got some disturbing news about Gypsum River Estuary.''

''Estuary?''

''You would probably call it a creek. It is the principal source of water for the entire ranch,'' Wellington said.

''What about it?''

''One of my riders tells me it is dry.''

''Does it sometimes run dry?''

''It floods and recedes, but it is never completely dry,'' Wellington said. ''And with all the recent rain and runoff, it should be in freshet stage right now.''

''I've seen beaver completely shut down a stream. We'll go take a look,'' Win said.

Joe stood up then, his hands covered with grease. ''Let me get some of this off, and I'll go with you,'' he said.

''No, you go ahead and finish the job,'' Win suggested. ''We're just going to take a look, that's all.''

When they left a few minutes later, Pamela was with them. She took great pride in describing the improvements her father had made to the land.

''Gypsum River was little more than a seasonal bayou when we came here,'' she explained. ''But Father connected the low spots and diverted the creek so that water began to follow what may have been an ancient riverbed. The result is a daily water flow that has provided sufficient water, not only for our ranch, but for all the ranches below us as well.''

''That must be the creek just ahead,'' Win said, pointing to a long line of dark green that cut through the land.

''You've a good eye about you, Mr. Coulter,'' Wellington said. ''That is it, indeed.''

When they reached the line of vegetation a few minutes later, Win saw that they were looking down on a channel that, while obviously much larger, had dwindled down to a tiny stream of water no more than a few inches wide and a few inches deep.

''My word!'' Wellington said, getting down from his horse and walking up to the edge of what had been the creek. ''Look at this.''

"Let's go upstream and see if we can find out what happened," Win suggested.

The three riders followed the dry streambed along its meandering course for better than five miles. Then, on the other side of a thick-growing patch of woods, they saw a large dam.

"What in the world?" Wellington gasped. "When and how did that get here?"

"It's no beaver dam, that's for sure," Win said.

"Look at the size of it, Father. It had to take whoever built it some time to do it. Why didn't we know about it?"

"We have no stock on this part of the range," Wellington replied. "And no reason to be here. Like as not they got the entire dam built, then closed the floodgates. We never realized it until the water flow stopped."

"Is that on your property?" Win asked.

"Actually, that is not," Wellington admitted. "My property line ends there, with the edge of that copse. From there on, it becomes part of Chad Emmerline's ranch, the Double-Diamond. But the water the dam has captured should be flowing on my property, and thus I consider it an invasion of my estate."

Wellington, Win, and Pamela crossed over the property line, then rode up to the dam and dismounted. A man, dressed in a business suit, walked over toward them. He was accompanied by two men, one a big man carrying a rifle, and another much smaller, but because of his strange chalky skin, his clear eyes, and the almost demonic expression on his face much more dangerous-looking.

"You are trespassing on government property," the man said.

"Government property? I thought this was Double-Diamond land. Who the devil are you, anyway?" Wellington demanded.

"The name is Canby, Harper Canby," the man replied. He pointed to the larger of the two armed men with him. "This is Mr. O'Lee, one of my assistants. The other gentleman is Mr. Shardeen, actually an employee of the Double-Diamond. Mr. Emmerline has graciously agreed to provide one of his own people to guard the government's interest here.''

"What government?" Wellington asked.

"Why, the U.S. Government, of course. I am one of their agents. And you are correct in assuming that this is Double-Diamond land, but the government has a lease arrangement with Mr. Emmerline, which allowed us to build this dam."

"Yes, well, that is the crux of the whole matter, isn't it?" Wellington sputtered in anger. "Why in heaven's name did you dam up Gypsum River?"

"We did it for the public good," Canby answered.

"And what public good is coming from this?" Wellington asked.

"Water improvement," Canby said.

"Improvement? Why, you bloody rascal, you have squeezed dry every drop of water from my ranch! And not only my ranch, but those ranches below me who are also dependent upon the Gypsum as a source of water."

"While I agree that it might appear that way, Mr. Wellington, in fact what we have done here is all for the common good," Canby said. Canby took a folded piece of paper from his inside jacket pocket. "I'm glad you came here today. It will allow me to serve you with this assessment for fifteen thousand dollars."

"Assessment for fifteen thousand dollars?" Wellington asked, frowning as he took the paper from Canby. "What the bloody hell are you talking about?"

"You and all the other ranchers are being assessed to pay for the water improvement work we have done," Canby said.

Wellington read the paper, then began to cough and sputter so that Win was afraid, for a moment, that he might be suffering from some sort of an attack.

"Have you gone mad?" Wellington bellowed. "First you steal my water, and then, to add insult to injury, you tell me that I must pay for the privilege. Why, that is an outrage! I have no intention of paying this assessment!"

"I'm afraid you have no choice, Wellington. You will either pay it, or we'll confiscate your land and cattle, and sell it for the monies due us. That is the law."

"You'll do no such thing," Wellington said. "In fact, if you don't tear this dam down, I will!"

Wellington shoved Canby aside and started toward the dam, but before he had taken three steps, O'Lee hit the Englishman with his rifle, not a skull-smashing blow, but a short, vicious chop, hard enough to drop Wellington like a sack of potatoes.

"Father!" Pamela shouted, going quickly to him.

"You son of a bitch!" Win swore. He took a step toward O'Lee, but Shardeen already had his own gun in his hand, cocked.

"You take one more step, mister, and you are a dead man," Shardeen said. Knowing that the ugly little maggot of a man meant what he said, Win stopped.

"You could have killed him!" Pamela said from her kneeling position by her father.

"Yes, we could have, but we didn't," Canby said. "And now, if you know what's good for you, you'll get your father on his feet and out of here. As I told you, you are trespassing on government property."

Wellington, who had gone out for just a moment, came to with a groan.

"Are you all right, Mr. Wellington?" Win asked.

"Yes, I think so," Wellington replied, rubbing the back of his head. When he brought his hand around to look at it, there was blood on his fingers.

"Mr. Wellington, you must accept my apology," Canby offered. "It is not the policy of the U.S. Government to assault people. But it is the policy to protect its property, and my deputy thought you intended to harm the dam."

"I do intend to harm it," Wellington said. "And I will bring it down, whatever it takes."

"I'm sorry to hear you reacting that way, Mr. Wellington," Canby said. "Because, of course, we can't allow that. And I'm afraid we must insist upon your paying your just assessment. You have thirty days, Mr. Wellington. Thirty days, or we will take further action against you."

"I'll be back," Wellington promised.

"If you do come back, Wellington, might I suggest you get a pass from the district office in Loraine? Otherwise, you will be trespassing and you could get shot."

6

BY THE TIME WIN, PAMELA, AND WELLINGTON RETURNED to the ranch, Wellington had grown nauseous and dizzy from the effects of the blow to his head. He was so unsteady in his saddle that for the last few miles Win had to lead his horse so Wellington could hang on. When they stopped in front of the house, Win dismounted quickly and helped Wellington from his saddle. Bascomb, seeing what was going on, came out quickly to offer a hand.

"What is wrong with His Lordship?" Bascomb asked.

"He's been hit in the head," Win said.

"Oh, my. Sir, would you help me get him to his room?"

"Yes, of course," Win said.

"Don't make such a fuss," Wellington mumbled. "I'll be all right."

Wellington took a few steps, then collapsed. Bascomb and Win picked him up and, as an anxious Pamela hurried alongside, carried him into the house.

"I don't understand," she said. "He didn't seem this badly hurt at first."

"I've seen it before," Win said. "People will take a blow to the head and at first seem all right. Then the wound begins to swell. I don't know, it must put pressure on the brain or something, because it gets worse."

"Could it be . . . fatal?" Pamela asked anxiously.

"Sometimes it is," Win admitted. When he saw the anxiousness on her face turn to fear, he added, "Although most of the time it isn't. And your father's wound doesn't seem that bad. Probably all he needs is a day or two to rest up."

A few minutes later, after Wellington was in bed and under the watchful care of his two faithful servants, Win started asking Pamela some questions.

"Your father said you have been having trouble with cattle rustlers, but he didn't say anything about trouble with the federal government."

Pamela shook her head. "That is what was so surprising about the incident today. Up until now, there had been no trouble with the federal government at all. All of our difficulties have been with rustlers."

"You know, I've been wanting to ask you about that as well. I realize that rustlers can be troublesome, but Camelot is a huge place, with thousands of cattle. It's hard to see how a few head of rustled cattle could cause so much trouble that your father seems actually concerned that he might lose the ranch."

"It's considerably more than a few head," Pamela said. "To date, we've lost over a thousand head."

Win whistled. "A thousand head? That's quite a job. I'm amazed anyone could steal that many cows and get away with it. I mean, how would a rustler, or a gang of rustlers, get rid of so many cows without being noticed?"

"That's the mystery none of us can understand, for we aren't the only ones suffering. All the other ranchers in the area are suffering crippling losses as well. Of course, no one else has lost as many head as we have, because we have the most to lose, except perhaps the Double-Diamond."

"Double-Diamond. That's the ranch we visited today, isn't it? Where the dam is."

"Yes, and it is nearly as large as Camelot. Especially since Chad Emmerline has been expanding his acreage by buying out the smaller ranchers. He's even offered to buy Camelot."

"Has Emmerline offered a fair price?"

"Who is to say? How does one put a price on a dream?" Pamela asked.

"Yes, but surely by now your father has learned that operating a big ranch is no picnic."

"Perhaps so, but Father isn't one to give up easily. Besides, where else could he go? He has no land, no home, no title back in England. When he left, all the bridges were burned behind him. No, we are here to stay, Win, whether he makes a go of it or is completely broken."

"Your father may wind up losing the ranch, but from what I have already seen of him, I don't think he will ever be broken," Win said. He looked back toward Wellington's bedroom. "Let him sleep now," he said. "That is the best thing for him."

Pamela reached out and put her hand on Win's, then squeezed it slightly.

"Thank you," she said.

LEAVING PHILLIP WELLINGTON IN GOOD HANDS, WIN went back out to the barn to join his brother. By now the wagon had been greased, a hay rake had been repaired, and a dozen other jobs attended to. Joe was just finishing straightening out some harness when Win stepped into the shadows of the machine shed.

"How is Mr. Wellington?" Joe asked.

"He'll be all right in a day or two," Win said. He looked around the shed, the interior of which was light and shadow, defined by the long, thin bars of light which slashed in through the cracks between the boards.

"You look like you've had a busy day," he said.

Joe smiled. "Yeah, I have," he said. He pointed to the shelves and tables of the machine shed. "It's been a while since anyone straightened things up in here. Why, Pa would've had a fit if we had kept our machine shed like this."

"You miss the farm, don't you, Joe?"

Joe put his hand on the leather traces of the harness he had just straightened out. "Yeah," he said. "I'd be lying to you if I told you I didn't miss it. But . . ." He sighed

before he went on. "I know we can't go back . . . even if
we were granted a full pardon in Missouri . . . we couldn't
go back."

Outside the shed they heard a couple of riders coming
in. Looking through the cracks between the boards, Win
saw that one of the riders was Cherokee.

"Ned, soon as you can, get on down to the breaks and
join the others," Cherokee said. "And don't say nothin'
'bout what we were doin'."

"You don't really think I'm dumb enough to, do you?"

"No, just bein' cautious, that's all," Cherokee replied.

"Sure hope they're not brandin'," Ned said. "I'm tired
of smellin' the stink."

"Give me the brandin' iron, I'll take care of it," Cherokee offered.

Ned handed the branding iron to Cherokee, then remounted and rode away. Cherokee started toward the machine shed, carrying the iron. Before he reached the shed,
Win and Joe stepped outside. Startled, Cherokee stopped.

"Afternoon," Win said.

"What the hell?" Cherokee asked, startled by their unexpected appearance. He looked back toward Ned, who was
already out of earshot. "Did you hear what we was talkin'
about?" he asked.

"No, should we have?" Win replied. He had heard the
admonition not to speak of what they had been doing, and
he found that curious, but he didn't know what it was about.

"No, it's none of your business," Cherokee said. He
pointed toward the machine shed. "What was you two
doin' in there?"

"Working," Joe answered. He pointed to the shed.
"Take a look for yourself, I've got everything straightened
up in there."

"Who told you to do that?" Cherokee growled.

"Nobody told me. I did it on my own."

"Mister, around here you don't do anything unless I tell
you to do it. I told you, I'm the foreman."

"It's a strange kind of foreman who doesn't appreciate

someone who is willing to work without being told,'' Win said.

"I like to know what's going on, that's all."

"You keep up with things, do you?" Win asked.

"That's a foreman's job."

"Then you no doubt will be interested to know that Mr. Wellington should recover from his injury."

"Injury?" Cherokee asked, genuinely surprised at the news. "What injury?"

"He was hit in the head by someone claiming to be a federal guard, down by the dam on Gypsum River."

"What dam on Gypsum River? There ain't no dam on Gypsum River."

"Yes, there is. The government leased some land from the Double-Diamond just across from Camelot's property line and built a dam there. Mr. Wellington, his daughter, and I visited it this morning," Win replied. "Being the good foreman you are, I would think you would've brought it to his attention before now."

"How was I supposed to know about it? I didn't know anything about a dam."

"You have noticed that Gypsum River is dry, haven't you?"

"So what? Streams fill and dry all the time out here."

Win shook his head. "I've been told that Gypsum River never runs dry. And even if it did, this is the wet season. Seems to me that, as the foreman, you would have noticed it before now."

"You tryin' to tell me how to do my job?" Cherokee asked.

"I'm not tryin' to tell you how to do your job," Win answered. "I'm just doin' my job."

"And what is your job?"

"The job Mr. Wellington hired me for," Win said. "To find out who's causing trouble for him."

"Yeah, well, just be careful that while you're findin' out who's causin' trouble for him, you ain't causin' trouble for me," Cherokee said.

"I'll be glad to," Win said. Then with a wry smile he

added, "Unless you're the one causing the trouble."

Cherokee glared at Win for a long moment, as if measuring his backbone. Then, determining that Win was someone who could back up what he said, Cherokee looked away.

"Why don't you let me put the brandin' iron away for you?" Joe asked, waiting until after Win had stared him down.

"Why don't you mind your own business?" Cherokee growled, jerking the iron away from him. "I'll put it away."

Cherokee strode angrily toward the machine shed while Joe and Win stood their ground, watching him walk away.

"Not a very likable cuss, is he?" Joe asked.

"No, I don't reckon he'll be invitin' us to share a bottle with him," Win agreed.

Joe chuckled.

JUST AFTER BREAKFAST THE NEXT MORNING, WIN WALKED down to the corral to watch the cowboys saddle their broncs and ride off by twos, threes, and sometimes larger groups, to attend to their assigned tasks.

Win had learned a lot about people over the last few years, and he wanted to look into the face of each rider as they left. If Wellington's problems were coming from within the ranks of his own employees, an expression or a look might provide Win with a clue.

His experiment bore no fruit, however, and when the last rider had left, Win rejoined Joe, who had been engaged in the same task, though from a different part of the corral.

"Did you see or hear anything suspicious?" Win asked.

"No," Joe said. "Just seemed like a bunch of guys goin' to work is all."

"Yeah," Win agreed. "Either none of them are involved, or the ones who are, are damned good at keepin' secrets."

At that moment a buckboard turned off the road and came up the long drive. There were two people in the buckboard, an older man and a very attractive young woman.

The woman was driving, and she pulled the team to a halt.

"Lordy, will you look at that?" Joe said, looking at the woman with obvious appreciation. "You ever see anyone any prettier than that woman?"

Win chuckled. "She's a looker, all right," he said. "I'll go see who she is and what she wants."

Joe cleared his throat. "Maybe I'd better go with you," he suggested.

The two brothers walked over to the buckboard, touching their hats in greeting as they approached.

"Howdy," Joe said, smiling broadly at the woman. Even though she was sitting down, he could see that she was tall. Her long red hair cascaded down across her shoulders, and her blue-green eyes looked out from above high cheekbones. She returned Joe's smile.

"You must be new here," she said. "I don't believe I've seen you before."

"I'm Joe Coulter. This is my brother, Win. We just started here a couple of days ago."

"I'm Julie Vincent. This is my uncle Seth," the girl replied. "We're Mr. Wellington's neighbors. We just learned that he was hurt yesterday. How is he?"

"You'll have to ask my brother that," Joe said. "He was with him when it happened."

"It could've been worse," Win said. "But he's much better this morning."

"Thank God for that," Julie said.

"Is it true?" the man with her asked. "Has the damn fool federal government dammed up Gypsum River?"

"Yes, sir, they have," Win said.

"What could they possibly have been thinking to do that?"

Win stroked his chin. "Your place must be downstream from Camelot," he said. "I take it the dam is going to be as bad for you as it is for Mr. Wellington."

"Not just as bad, Mr. Coulter," Julie said. "It will be much worse. Camelot has a few other sources of water. The Flying V has only a few ponds here and there, and they will dry up when the summer is at its height. I don't know what we'll do then.''

Pamela, having seen Julie and her uncle arrive, came out of the house to meet them. After warm greetings, the three went back into the house.

''I don't know about you, Big Brother, but in my mind, that is one good-lookin' woman,'' Joe said.

''She sure is. And I'm even getting used to her accent.''

''Accent? What accent?''

''Her English accent.''

''Who the hell is talking about Miss Wellington? I'm talking about Julie Vincent.''

7

THREE DAYS LATER, WHEN WELLINGTON WAS FULLY RE-
covered, he called a meeting of all the ranchers whose land
was affected by the "water improvements." Win, Joe, and
the cowboys who weren't out on the range watched the
ranchers, big and small, arriving for the meeting in various
means of conveyances: buckboards, democrat wagons,
open stages, phaetons, country wagons, traps, and, of
course, horses. Vehicles and livestock filled the curved
driveway as the ranchers went into the house and gathered
in Wellington's large living room. By now, all knew about
the dam and most had been assessed payment by the government. Though Wellington's 15,000 dollars was the high-
est amount, the others, less affluent, were proportionately
just as badly hurt.

"Clyde, I was real sorry to hear about Dooley and
Snake," Tony Kindig, another rancher, said.

"Dooley and Snake?" Wellington repeated. "Aren't
they the two young men who used to work for me?"

"Yes," Clyde Carter said.

Wellington chuckled. "What did they do? Get a bit
rowdy in town and wind up in the lockup?"

"They got themselves killed."

Wellington was surprised by the answer. "Killed? My
word! How did that happen?"

"They were goaded into a fight in the Black Horse Saloon in town," Clyde explained. "And they were shot down."

"Heavens, I hope the authorities have the murderer under arrest."

Clyde sighed. "According to the witnesses, it wasn't murder, it was a fair fight. Though how you can call a gunfight between two working cowboys like Dooley and Snake and a paid killer like Shardeen fair, I'll never know."

"Did you say the fellow who shot them was named Shardeen?"

"Yes. Lucas Shardeen, the infamous gunman. I'm sure you've heard of him."

"No, I've never heard of him. But I have met him."

"You met him?"

"Yes. Odd-looking chap, he was. A true albino. You don't see many of those."

"Albino, yeah, that's him, all right. They say his eyes is as clear as glass."

"What was he doing out at the dam?" Seth asked.

"I think he was providing some sort of guard duty. I was told that he is in the employ of Chad Emmerline."

"Let me get this straight. He is workin' for Chad Emmerline, but he was standin' guard over a government dam?"

"Yes, that appeared to be the case," Wellington replied.

"Boys, if we needed any proof that Emmerline was behind all this, that should be it," Clyde said.

"Yeah, well, Emmerline ain't hurtin' none, that's for sure. Fact is, he's still buyin' land from those who will sell to him," one of the owners said.

"That's true," Tony agreed. "He's made me an offer for my land." He paused for a moment before he went on. "And I have to tell you boys, I think I'm goin' to take him up on it."

"What did he offer you, Tony?" Wellington asked.

"He's offered me to buy my stock at ninety percent of the market price, give me two and a half dollars an acre for my land, and he'll pay the assessment charges himself."

"Two and a half dollars an acre?" Wellington scoffed. "Why, Tony, your land's worth twenty times that and you know it!"

"It's worth that with water," Tony agreed. "But without water, that dirt ain't doin' nothin' but holdin' the world together. Hell, if it wasn't for the fact that Emmerline has been lettin' my cows onto his rangeland for water, they'd all be dyin'."

"You mean Emmerline is letting your stock water on his range?" someone asked.

"Yeah," Tony answered. Then he added, "But he's takin' every third cow for payment."

"Every third cow? My God, that's what he's askin'?" Seth exclaimed. He shook his head. "And here I was, thinking about going to him, hat in hand, to see if I could work out a deal. But, every third cow?"

"Tell me, Mr. Vincent, you do agree that keeping two thirds of your herd is better than letting all of your cows die of thirst, don't you?" a new voice suddenly asked. "And when you consider that I have a rather large herd of my own to look after . . . perhaps you'll realize that my offer is fair."

Wellington and his guests looked toward the door of the parlor. What they saw standing there was a man who had no hair of any kind; no eyebrows, and no eyelashes. Even his chin was smooth-skinned as a woman's.

"Yeah, well, what is it costing you, Emmerline?" Clyde asked with a growl. "You got more water now than ever before. Hell, we all know that you're the only one who benefited from this Yankee government water project."

"That's true, I have benefited," Emmerline admitted easily. He looked at Wellington. "Phillip, I know that I wasn't invited to this meeting, but I hope my presence isn't unwelcome. If it is, I shall move on without delay."

"Of course you are welcome here, Chad," Wellington said graciously. "I hope you don't consider your omission a slight. It's just that since you aren't facing the same water problem the rest of us are, I thought you wouldn't be interested."

"Nonsense," Emmerline said. "If my good friends and neighbors are hurt, then so am I. I want us to find some way to resolve it, if we can."

"Do you have any suggestions, Mr. Emmerline?" one of the other ranchers asked.

"Yeah," another put in. "Can you tell us how to get our water back?"

"I'm afraid I have no answer to that problem, gentlemen," Emmerline replied. "Although I did discuss this very matter with Mr. Canby at some length. I even asked him if he would remove the dam, or at least install a sluice to allow a measured amount of water through. But he turned me down. Apparently the government is quite committed to improving the water system for this part of the country."

"Improving the water system?" Wellington said. "You know, I do believe that is the most disturbing aspect of this entire bizarre affair. How could anyone possibly call this dam an improvement?"

Emmerline removed a pipe from his jacket pocket and began stuffing the bowl with tobacco.

"Well, Phillip," he said calmly, all the while tamping down the tobacco, "I can see why such a thing might get you riled. But we have to take a look at the long-range view of this operation. When I spoke with Mr. Canby, he told me that if the water system isn't improved, the time will come when this whole basin will be as dry as a desert. Now, we certainly don't want that, do we?"

"Hell, the Yankee sons of bitches are turning it into a desert now!" one of the ranchers protested angrily.

"Be that as it may, gentlemen, it *is* a government project and, as such, we are not able to get it changed. But my offer still stands to all who would want to take advantage of it. You may lease water rights from me in exchange for one third of your cattle."

"That brings us back to where we were when you came in," Wellington said. "Isn't that rather steep?"

"If you don't want to do that, you can sell your land to me," Emmerline suggested.

"At two dollars and fifty cents an acre?" one of the ranchers asked.

"It's a fair price, under the circumstances," Emmerline insisted.

"You already know my answer, Mr. Emmerline," Tony said. "I am accepting your offer."

"Yes, Tony, and I appreciate your vote of confidence," Emmerline replied.

"Tony, won't you reconsider?" Wellington asked.

Tony shook his head. "Look, I know when I'm licked. If I don't sell at two and a half per acre now, I'll be lucky to get twenty-five cents an acre for it by the end of summer. I really don't have any choice."

"What about you, Phillip?" Emmerline asked.

"I'm not interested in selling my land," Wellington said.

"I know. I was speaking about my offer to water your herd."

"For one third?"

"That's my price."

"You are asking me to turn over a minimum of ten thousand cows to you. At twenty-five dollars a head that's a quarter of a million dollars, just for water rights!"

"Yes, it is," Emmerline replied easily.

"Well, I won't do it," Wellington insisted. "I can't do it!"

"I'm sorry you feel that way," Emmerline said. "For a thirst-maddened herd the size of yours could be quite dangerous."

"We haven't reached that point yet," Wellington said. "Although Gypsum River is my primary source of water supply, I do have some other sources."

"You're talking about Frog Creek?"

"Yes, I'm talking about Frog Creek."

"Well, Frog Creek is running now," Emmerline said. "But it will be bone-dry by the end of August, and then you will be in the same boat as everyone else. What will you do then?"

"We have a saying for that in my country," Wellington

said. "Perhaps you have heard it. 'That bridge shall be negotiated when it is reached.' "

"Phillip, I hate to say this," one of the other ranchers said. "But Emmerline is right. If we don't make some sort of agreement with him, we stand to lose everything."

"We've got to do something," another said.

"All right, but not this," Wellington pleaded. "Don't sell out everything that you have worked for."

"Have you got any better ideas?"

"I don't know yet, but I'm thinking about it," Wellington said. "And I will come up with something."

"That's fine for you, Mr. Wellington, you are a wealthy man and you can afford the loss. Plus you have Frog Creek. I know that ain't much water, but if it wasn't for a few ponds left over from the rain, we wouldn't have no water at all."

"I'll share my water with you," Wellington offered.

"Phillip, you can't do that, you barely have enough for your own stock," Seth said.

Wellington waved his hand as if dismissing Seth's precaution. "It doesn't matter," he said. "We are all in this together. We'll find a solution together . . . or we'll go down together."

The other ranchers applauded.

"Very commendable, Phillip," Emmerline said. "And I wish you well. Oh, before I leave, I would like to remind you gentlemen that I am hosting a barbecue for all the working cowboys at my ranch tomorrow. It's my way of expressing appreciation to them for the thankless job they do for all of us. And whether you, personally, are prepared to do any business with me or not, I do hope you will at least allow your hired hands to attend."

"I've only got four hands left," Seth said. "But I think they're plannin' on being there."

"Same goes for my boys," another said.

"Two of mine won't be there," Clyde said dryly. "Them bein' Snake Anders and Dooley Morgan."

"Yes, I know about those two," Emmerline said. "They should've known better than to try and brace a professional

gunman, but you know how it is with young men like that
. . . they get a few drinks in them, and it is my understanding they were showing off in front of a prostitute who
worked in the saloon. Still, it is regrettable and I expressed
my feelings about it to Shardeen. He has assured me that
he will go out of his way to avoid any such confrontations
in the future."

"Yes, I'm sure he'll be as meek as a Sunday school
teacher," Clyde growled.

"Gentlemen, I seem to have disturbed the equanimity of
your gathering. If you will excuse me, I'll take my leave
now."

"You mark my words," Clyde said after Emmerline was
gone. "Somehow that son of a bitch got the government to
build that dam. I don't know how he did it, but he did it
as sure as a gun is iron."

The meeting broke up shortly after Emmerline left, and,
though nothing concrete had been resolved, Wellington's
offer to share his diminishing water supply with those who
already had none gave the ranchers a little more hope and
resolve. Even Tony suggested that he might not sell out
after all but would stick it out for a little longer. Then, in
twos and threes, the vehicles and horses started back down
the long, curved driveway, the first step of the journey back
to their own places.

Seth Vincent and his niece Julie accepted Wellington's
invitation to stay for supper and beyond, and, shortly after
the last visitor left, Bascomb came out to the tack room.
The tack room, or rather the small room behind it, was
where Win and Joe were making their quarters. If Cherokee
thought he was making it uncomfortable for Win and Joe
by banning them from the bunkhouse, he was mistaken.
For several years now, the two brothers had made their
home wherever they might find it, under the shelter of an
overhanging rock, in a cave, or a bedroll under the stars.
With its two beds, table and chairs, and kerosene lantern,
the tack house was pure luxury compared to their normal
quarters.

Win was sitting at the table, using the lantern light to

read a book he had borrowed from Wellington's library. Joe was sitting on the edge of his bed, carving on a forked stick, when Bascomb knocked on the open door, then stuck his head in.

"I beg your pardon, gentlemen," Bascomb said in his low-pitched, cultured voice.

"Yes, Bascomb, what is it?" Win asked.

"Lord Wellington is extending an invitation for the two of you to join him and Miss Wellington and their guests, the Vincents, for dinner."

"Julie Vincent?" Joe asked quickly, looking up from his carving.

"I believe that is the young lady's name," Bascomb replied.

"Hell yes, we'll go!" Joe said excitedly, without waiting for confirmation from Win. "Tell them we'll be there!"

"Very good, sir," Bascomb said as he withdrew.

Joe put down his forked stick and began going through his roll. Then, with a triumphant snort, he pulled out a pair of trousers.

"There they are!" he said. "I knew I had a clean pair."

"Clean pants and a clean shirt? What is bringing on this sudden display of vanity, as if I didn't know?" Win teased.

"It don't hurt to look good ever' now an' then," Joe said. "Listen, you 'member that bottle of bay rum I bought back in Austin? You seen it anywhere?"

"You used it all up as a mosquito repellent, didn't you?"

"Shit, that's right," Joe said. "Damn me for a fool. I shoulda saved some of it."

Win chuckled. "Well, hell, Little Brother, if it'll ward off mosquitoes, what makes you think it won't ward off Miss Vincent?"

"Yeah," Joe agreed. "Yeah, maybe you got a point there." He felt his rough chin. "Well, the least I can do is shave."

HALF AN HOUR LATER BOTH BROTHERS, WASHED AND freshly shaved, wearing clean shirts and clean trousers, though without the benefit of any bay rum, once again found themselves at the dinner table in Wellington's posh dining room. Joe, by his own manipulation, was sitting next to Julie. Win was next to Pamela. Phillip Wellington and Seth Vincent were sitting at opposite ends of the table.

"I could trim my herd, I suppose," Wellington said. "Cut it back by about a third. That would make the water go a bit farther."

"What about when the water dries up?" Seth asked.

"Yes, well, it's only completely dry for about a month and a half," Wellington replied.

"You think any cow on this range is going to survive forty-five days without water?"

"Probably not, but I don't have any idea what else to do."

"Why don't you dig some wells?" Joe asked easily. He pointed to the platter of biscuits.

Wellington looked at Joe as if he were answering the suggestion of a child.

"Wells would be wonderful, of course," he said. "But, where to dig them?"

"Would you mind if I had another three or four of them biscuits? They're awful good."

"My, you do have an appetite, Mr. Coulter," Julie said, reaching for the platter.

"Yes'm, I reckon I do," Joe admitted. "Mr. Wellington, if there is a natural supply of water aboveground, then there's water underground."

"Yes, an aquifer," Wellington said. "I am quite familiar with the concept. Still, the question remains, where do you dig them? You can't just go out there and dig a hole anywhere and hope to find water. And even if you did, how would you get it out of the ground?"

"Getting it out of the ground is easy," Win replied. "All you have to do is put in some windmills."

"Windmills? Good heavens, you mean like those huge monstrosities one finds in Holland?"

"Holland? Where's that?" Joe asked, putting butter on one of his biscuits. "Don't think I've ever been there. That up north, somewhere?"

"Holland is a country, over in Europe," Win explained. "No, Mr. Wellington, I've seen pictures of the windmills they have in Holland. I'm not talking about anything like that. The windmills we would use are quite small compared to that. There are little more than wooden frames, upon which blades are mounted. The blades spin in the wind, and in turning operate a pump. The pump will bring up the water and fill a trough. If you have enough of those placed about your ranch, then it won't matter if you never get Gypsum River back. And if you set the example, I'm sure all the other ranchers would do the same thing."

"Yes, that would be wonderful," Wellington agreed. "But you haven't answered the most important question. How will we find the water?"

"Oh, you don't have to worry about that," Joe said, taking half the biscuit with one bite. He chewed thoughtfully. "I'll find it for you."

Julie laughed. "You'll find it?" she asked.

"Yep."

"And just how do you propose to do that?" Wellington asked.

"By dowsing for it," Joe answered. "I've already cut myself a dowsing stick. It's a good one too."

"A dowsing stick?" Wellington asked, his face a mask of confusion. "What in the blazes is a dowsing stick?"

"Some folks call 'em divining rods. I used them all the time back in Missouri, before the war. We had three wells on the family farm, and I found all three of 'em."

"He also found wells on several other farms," Win added. "My brother's the best dowser I ever saw. Don't worry about where the water is, Mr. Wellington. Joe'll find it for you."

"I appreciate the offer," Wellington said dismissively. "But I would not like to put my faith in witchcraft."

"This here ain't witchcraft," Joe said, the expression on his face showing that he was hurt by the accusation. "It's a science."

"Father, I think we should let him try it," Pamela said. "After all, what do we have to lose?"

"She's got you there, Phillip," Seth agreed. "All in the world can happen is the boy will either find water or he won't. If he does find it, it could be the solution to our problem. And if he doesn't find it, well, then we are no worse off than we are now."

Wellington was silent for a moment, then his face broke into a big grin. "Of course you are right," he said. "We won't lose anything by trying. All right, Mr. Coulter, I accept your kind offer. When would you like to do it?"

"How about tomorrow?"

"Tomorrow will be fine."

"Wait," Pamela said. "What about the barbecue Mr. Emmerline is giving for all the cowboys tomorrow?"

"What barbecue?" Win asked.

"Emmerline was just here," Wellington explained. "Evidently, he is hosting some sort of appreciation for the working class tomorrow. He has invited all the hands from all the neighboring ranches to attend something he calls a barbecue."

"And having observed your appetite firsthand," Pamela said, smiling, "I'm sure you wouldn't want to miss out on the opportunity to have a free meal."

"I know!" Julie said. "If you stay here and dowse, we'll have our own picnic. That is, if it's all right with you, Pamela," she added quickly.

"Why, I think that would be a wonderful idea," Pamela answered. "A dowsing and a picnic. Who could ask for a more entertaining day?"

8

WIN WAITED UNTIL HIS BROTHER WAS ASLEEP BEFORE HE responded to the note Pamela had slipped to him as they were leaving. The note read:

Mr. Coulter, my room is the one at the left rear corner of the house. And as my windows open onto a big cottonwood tree, one who is both agile and ambitious might find a way to gain entry without being seen. Would you know of such a person?

With Joe's snores renting the air behind him, Win left the tack room, moved quietly along the corral fence, then waited until the moon slipped behind a cloud before dashing quickly across the open area to the large cottonwood tree. A moment later he was crawling out on the limb that reached over toward her windows. He was about to step down onto the mansard roof when he heard Pamela's quiet voice coming from the dark.

"No, the wood is rotten there. Come on out on the limb a few feet farther."

Win pulled his foot back, crawled a few feet farther out onto the limb, then looked up. Though it was dark in the room, he could see her standing just inside the window.

Was she naked?

At first he wasn't sure, because he had only the soft, silver glow of the moon by which to see her. But when she reached out toward him, as if to help him through the window, she turned slightly, causing her body to be highlighted by light and shadow. At that moment the question was resolved.

Pamela was completely, gloriously, and beautifully nude.

Win gave out a little gasping sound, a quick intake of breath, for he had never seen anything more inviting.

"I wasn't sure you would come," she said as he stepped through the open window into her bedroom.

"I'd be a fool to turn down an invitation like the one you gave me," Win answered, smiling at her.

"I know you must consider me a brazen hussy," Pamela said. "First by sending you the note, and then by meeting you like this."

Win reached toward her firm, round breasts. "I can't think of any way I would rather be met," he said. He brushed his lips across the nipples, moving from one to the other.

Pamela's body twitched, and Win felt her muscles tighten. She brought her hands up to the sides of his head and guided him from side to side. Then, even as he was kissing her breasts and sucking her nipples, he was undoing his trousers and pushing them and his underwear down to the floor.

Pamela helped him get undressed, then she grabbed his swelling shaft and squeezed it.

"Oh, my," she breathed. "You are . . . uh . . . very much a man!"

Win picked her up and carried her over to the bed, but when he put her on her back, she shook her head and sat up again.

"No," she said.

"I thought you wanted to do this," Win started, surprised by her resistance to the move.

"I do" she said. "But not yet, not until we've had a little fun first."

"I *was* having fun," Win said. "I mean, I couldn't ask for more . . . oh . . . oh, yes, I see what you mean," he gasped.

The change in his tone was brought about by Pamela dropping her head to take his shaft into her moist, warm mouth. He put his hands on the back of her head, running his fingers through her hair as she began using her mouth, working her jaws in and out, decreasing and increasing the pressure by sucking, and, most stimulating of all, by using her tongue to flick, caress, and tease him, to bring him close.

"No," he finally rasped. "I don't want to finish this way."

"You don't like it?" she asked, pulling him just far enough out to be able to speak. He looked down at her as she held his cock pressed against her lips, as if she didn't want to let it get too far away from her.

"Yes, I do like it," he said. "But I like it more when I give you pleasure too."

Pamela laughed, a low, throaty laugh. "But you *are* giving me pleasure," she said. "It pleasures me to pleasure you."

"Let's try it my way," Win said. "See if you don't like it better."

Acquiescent to his demand, she got up, then lay on her back. Win bent his head to again caress her nipples with the tip of his tongue, and Pamela's hand replaced her mouth to stroke his engorged shaft. Finally, Win realized that he couldn't keep this up much longer, so he climbed over her, then let her guide him into her, driving deep inside her moist warmth with one, long thrust.

"Oh, yes," Pamela said. "It's wonderful!"

Win began stroking slowly with long, sensory-laden thrusts, holding it for just a moment at the point of its deepest penetration before pulling himself out and pushing in again.

Pamela clamped her legs around his hips and clung to him as he rose and fell, and each time he reached the bottom she cried out little moans of ecstasy.

Win continued with her, maintaining a steady pace, timing himself by listening to her moans and feeling the reaction from her body. Taking his cue from her he began, gradually, to speed up the tempo until they were no longer long, slow, deliberate strokes but hard, quick, pistonlike drives that changed her moans to short, sharp cries which she attempted to bury in his neck to keep from being overheard.

"Oh, yes, yes, yes," she was crying. "Oh, I want it, I want you! Win, yes, Win!"

Her words ran together into a sound that burst from her throat in one long, keening sob. As she cried out, she writhed and moaned, keeping her eyes shut while she shuddered in spasms of ecstasy.

Win, recognizing the urgency of her tone and the intensity in her movement, pounded against her with the full force of his body, driving on lustily, racing to his own climax, catching up with her as the final, smothered screams rose from her trembling throat. He reached his peak, then fell forward on her soft warm body as he squirted and drained himself into her, letting his muscles go limp while her final, throaty sighs of satisfaction sounded softly in his ears.

IN THE ROOM NEXT DOOR TO PAMELA'S, JULIE, WHO WAS a houseguest for the night, lay there for just a moment wondering what had awakened her. Then, as she heard the rhythmic creaking of bedsprings accompanied by the staccato squeals, she realized what it was.

She was embarrassed at first, then devilishly curious. To her surprise, though, that curiosity was soon replaced by yet another sensation as her heartbeat quickened and a warmth began to spread through her. She couldn't stop herself from listening intently.

"Oh," Pamela moaned again. And then the "ohs" turned to little screams of pleasure, and the sound of the thrashing bedsprings grew more frenzied, and a man's moans began to mingle with the woman's.

Julie kicked the covers off as she began to perspire. She was mortified by her reaction, but she was helpless to control it.

Finally the man and the woman moaned in unison, a

long, loud moan, and their cries and the sounds of the straining bed stopped. For several seconds there was total silence.

Julie just lay there, so self-conscious that she could almost feel the blood moving in her veins. Her body tingled all over, from the soles of her feet to her scalp. For one irrational moment she was afraid she'd been caught eavesdropping, but she knew that couldn't be. She wondered who Pamela's mystery lover was. She was certain it was one of the Coulter brothers, but she hoped it wasn't the big one. She had her own designs on him.

Then, thinking about Joe, and wishing that he had come to visit her, she finally, fitfully, dropped off to sleep again.

THE NEXT MORNING JOE COULTER WAS THE CENTER OF attention as he started out across a meadow, carrying his dowsing stick in front of him. Win, Wellington, Pamela, Julie, and Seth were walking behind him. Cherokee and a scattering of cowboys were behind them, all looking on in fascination as Joe walked in a zigzag pattern across the meadow.

"What's he doin'?" one of the cowboys asked.

"He's lookin' for water."

"With that stick? How's he goin' to find water with that stick?"

"He ain't."

"I don't know, I seen it done oncet," a cowboy named Pete said.

"You gettin' any sign, Joe?" Win asked after half an hour of dowsing.

"Not so much as a twitch," Joe replied. He lowered the forked stick, then pulled out a handkerchief to wipe the sweat from his brow.

"Maybe there's no water on the place," Win suggested.

"No, there's water here," Joe said.

"How do you know?" Cherokee asked.

"Because I can feel it," Joe replied.

Cherokee snorted a scoffing laugh. "Boys, we ain't ever goin' to be thirsty again," he said sarcastically. "The big fella here is goin' to find us all the water we need with that there stick.''

Several of the cowboys laughed.

"I think we should give him the opportunity to prove his experiment, Mr. Brown," Wellington said. "He just started."

"Yes, sir, well, me an' Ned has got some work to do, anyway," Cherokee replied. "We can't hang aroun' here all day."

"You want me and some of the other boys to come with you, Cherokee?" Pete asked.

"No, Pete, Ned and I can handle it just fine," Cherokee answered.

Pete cleared his throat then and looked around at his friends who, by the expressions on their faces, the nods, grimaces, winks, and jerks, were urging him to go on.

Pete cleared his throat again. "Uh, listen, Cherokee, then seein' as you don't need us, is it okay if me and several of the boys go on over to that barbecue they're ahavin' at the Double-Diamond?"

"Yeah, it's all right with me if it's all right with the boss," Cherokee replied, looking toward Wellington.

"No doubt Emmerline will use that opportunity to make an effort to hire you away from Camelot."

"He can make all the effort he wants. It ain't goin' to work with me, boss. I like it here," Pete said.

Wellington chuckled. "Very well, boys, if you gentlemen believe you can stand up to whatever enticement he may offer, then by all means, go and enjoy yourselves."

"Thanks, boss," Pete said, smiling broadly. "Come on, boys. They say they's goin' to be some women there."

Amidst a chorus of thank-yous and general expressions of appreciation and anticipation, the cowboys who had gathered to watch the dowsing now headed en masse toward the corral.

"Mr. Brown, are you sure you and Ned wouldn't like to go as well?" Wellington offered. "I'm sure that whatever you have to do can be put off a day."

"Nah, we can't go. If we don't get it done today it'll

just be that much more work when we do get around to it,'' Cherokee answered. ''I reckon we'd better see to it.''

''I admire your discipline,'' Wellington said. ''And I appreciate your dedication to duty. Lord knows what kind of trouble we would be in around here if you weren't foreman.''

''Well, sir, I believe in a day's work for a day's pay,'' Cherokee said. ''Come on, Ned. We have work to do.''

The other cowboys, by now saddled and whooping and laughing at each other over their anticipated day off, rode out, heading toward the Double-Diamond. Shortly after that Win saw Ned go into the toolshed and come out with a branding iron. Then he and Cherokee left as well, heading in the opposite direction.

''Phillip, much as I would like to watch this, I have to be getting back to my own place,'' Seth said. ''My own boys will, no doubt, be over at the Double-Diamond, and I think someone should be there to watch over things.''

''Yes, well, I've got some papers to take care of myself,'' Wellington said. ''And it is getting a little warm out here. Mr. Coulter, how long do you think it will be before you have some results?''

Joe lowered the divining rod. ''Well, now, I couldn't tell you, Mr. Wellington. Sometimes the thing just about jumps out of my hand, sometimes you don't get nothin' more'n a twitch or two. So far today I ain't got nothin' at all. I plan to keep on looking though.''

''I appreciate that,'' Wellington said. ''But you understand, you're under no obligation to find water. That wasn't part of our agreement.''

''I know it wasn't,'' Joe said. ''But if there's water here, and I believe there is, then I plan to find it for you.''

''You haven't forgotten, have you, Mr. Vincent, that we are going to have our own picnic here?'' Pamela asked.

''You young people go on and have it without me,'' Seth invited. ''Julie, you'll find a way home?''

''Yes, Uncle Seth,'' Julie replied. ''I'm sure Mr. Coulter would escort me.'' She looked directly at Joe as she spoke.

''Yes, sir, I'd be very pleased to take your niece home,''

Joe said, quick to take advantage of the opportunity that had just presented itself. He had no idea that Pamela and Julie had already "divided the spoils" this morning, each laying out her claim for the Coulter she would go after. That conversation had taken place shortly after Julie learned, to her relief, that Pamela's night visitor was Win and not Joe.

"Well, then, it's all settled," Julie said. "Unless you have some objection," she added, looking toward her uncle.

Seth held up his hand and chuckled. "You two ladies seem to have planned this like some military operation," he said. "I wouldn't think of raising an objection."

9

IT TOOK AN HOUR OF STEADY RIDING BEFORE CHEROKEE and Ned reached their destination, an arroyo which Wellington and all the others on the ranch believed was a dead-end canyon. It wasn't dead-end at all, but had a deceptive aperture which, though hard to find, provided a way for horse, rider, and even cattle, if carefully driven, to pass through the arroyo then emerge into a hidden valley on the other side.

The pass was a narrow chasm, masked by a high-standing needle rock. It was a ragged vent in the walls of red stone. The first five hundred feet was difficult enough going that it discouraged all but the most hardy, then it opened into a wide, flat field some twenty or so acres in size. Water was not natural to the canyon, but the recent damming of Gypsum River had diverted a stream here that was wide enough and deep enough to supply the needs of almost a thousand head.

There was grass too, though not enough to last very long. There was just enough grass to sustain the cattle until the re-branding had been completed and they were taken out the other side.

There were half a dozen cowboys camping near the assembled herd, and they came over to greet Cherokee and Ned as they arrived.

"If you'd leave that brandin' iron here, we could move a lot faster," one of them suggested.

"Not on your life," Cherokee growled. "My deal with Emmerline is that I get five dollars for every head I turn over to him with the Double-Diamond brand. And the only way I can keep an accurate count is if I brand them myself."

"Are you sayin' we ain't honest? You think we might cheat you?"

Cherokee snorted. "Hell, Gibbons, you're a goddamn cow thief. How dishonest can you get? Yes, I'm sayin' you might cheat me. Now come on, let's get started."

"We got a hundred or so head penned up over there, ready to start," Gibbons said.

Cherokee took the W branding iron with him and went over to lay it in the fire. A moment later, when the W at the end of the iron was gleaming red, he nodded, and one of the cows was brought over to him and held. Cherokee picked up the branding iron and, inverting the red-hot W above the branded W which was already on the cow's hide, stuck the iron against the cow's flesh. The cow bawled and jumped, and the smell of smoke and burned animal flesh assailed the nostrils.

When Cherokee pulled the branding iron away, the two opposing W's had become two diamonds. The cow, which a moment earlier had sported the W brand of Camelot, was now clearly wearing the identity of a cow belonging to Chad Emmerline's Double-Diamond spread.

"There you go, fellas," Cherokee said. "That's another five dollars Emmerline owes me."

Ned laughed. "Just think, in no more'n thirty seconds, you earned enough money to take one of Ginny's girls upstairs with you for a whole night."

"That'll sure be a change for you, Ned," one of the rustlers said. "Most of the time you work a whole night to be able to take one of Ginny's girls upstairs with you for thirty seconds."

Cherokee and the rustlers laughed.

• • •

"YOU WANT TO KNOW SOMETHIN' CURIOUS, JOE?" WIN asked. Win and his brother were alone in the meadow, still walking back and forth across it, waiting for the divining rod to make its mysterious dip.

"What's that?"

"Well, I'm the first to admit that I don't know much about ranchin', but it's curious to me that Cherokee and Ned would have so much branding to do at this time of the year. Seems to me like the only time they'd be doing any serious branding is right after calving."

"Yeah," Joe said. "Well, it can't be all that serious or he'd a taken some more men with him. Must just be a few mavericks here and there."

"I suppose you're right. Still, it makes you wonder why he's willin' to do it himself instead of givin' the job to someone else."

"Well, don't forget the barbecue. Maybe he's just a nice guy and he figured to do the work himself so the other boys could go over to the Double-Diamond."

Win laughed. "Cherokee a nice guy? Yeah, and pigs fly."

As promised, when noon came around, Pamela and Julie came out to the meadow to join them, bringing a picnic lunch in a hamper. They came without Wellington, not because he wasn't asked, but because he was smart enough to get the broad hint that his company really wasn't expected . . . or wanted. The two women spread a cloth out on the ground, then opened the basket to display a couple of fried chickens, a pan of freshly baked biscuits, baked beans, coleslaw, and an apple pie.

Pamela was relatively quiet during the meal. That too was by design, for she and Julie had agreed that Julie would use this opportunity to "get better acquainted with Joe." Thus, during the discussion they learned that Julie's father had been killed during the war. As her mother had died many years before that, she had no place to go except to Seth Vincent, who was her father's brother.

"He sounds like a good uncle," Joe said.

"Oh, he's been a wonderful uncle," Julie said. "But he's

much more than an uncle. He's like my mother and father as well."

AT THAT VERY MOMENT SETH WAS PULLING INTO THE front yard of his own ranch, his team lathered from the exertion of an all-out gallop for the last two miles. The dramatic entrance was because Seth had seen smoke climbing into the sky from a couple of miles back, and though he prayed hard that it be something else . . . he knew that it had to be his house. That fear was quickly borne out by the flames, which were licking high into the sky from a house that was now little more than fuel for the blazing inferno.

A short distance from the burning house, Seth saw a few saddled horses tied to a tree, and he jumped down from the wagon and ran toward them. There were two men standing near the horses, and he was shocked to see that one of them was Chad Emmerline.

"Emmerline, what are you doing?" Seth shouted. "Why are you just standing there, watching? Why aren't you trying to put it out!"

"Put it out? Now, why would we want to put it out, Mr. Vincent, when I am the one who started it?"

"What? Are you telling me you are the cause of this? Why? For God's sake, Emmerline! Why would you do such a thing?"

Chad Emmerline rubbed his hand across his bald head.

"It didn't have to be this way," he said. "You could've sold out to me."

"You . . . you bastard!" Seth said. "That's why you had your damned barbecue! You wanted to get my men away from here!"

"You're a smart man, Mr. Vincent. Isn't he a smart man, Shardeen?"

Shardeen! Seth looked around and saw a third man, one he had not seen earlier. He was small and bestially ugly, exactly fitting the description of the killer he had heard the others talking about at the meeting yesterday.

"You—you are the one who killed Clyde's two men," Seth said.

"You're right, Mr. Emmerline. He is a smart man," Shardeen said.

"Get off the Flying V, you sorry bastard," Vincent ordered. He looked over at Emmerline and the others. "All of you! Get off my property now."

"I'm afraid we can't do that," Emmerline said. "You see, you came back too early."

"What?"

"If you had come back later and found your house already burned, you might have sold out to me. But now that you know I am the one who burned it . . . Well, you can understand, can't you? I'm afraid this changes everything."

Suddenly Seth realized what Emmerline was saying. Emmerline was telling him that he was about to die.

Seth's anger was replaced by a cold, gripping fear. He made an urgent grab for his pistol, but Shardeen had been watching and waiting for this precise moment. With an evil smile Shardeen pulled his pistol and had it out and leveled at Seth before Seth could even clear his holster. Seeing that he was beaten, Seth stopped in mid-draw and started to put his gun back. "All right, you win," he said.

"Uh-uh, it don't work that way," Shardeen said. He pulled the trigger, the gun roared, and a finger of flame stabbed toward Seth.

Seth felt a heavy blow to his chest, then a numbness, then nothing.

"WHAT DO YOU WANT TO DO WITH HIM?" THE OTHER MAN with Emmerline and Shardeen asked.

"We'll take him over behind the barn and leave him there," Emmerline suggested.

"Hey, boss, if this guy is dead, how will you ever get this land signed over to you?" the man wanted to know. He had to struggle alone under the weight of Seth's body, for neither Emmerline nor Shardeen offered to help.

"The ranch will now pass on to his niece," Emmerline said. "And I'm quite sure she won't be so stubborn."

• • •

FOR JOE AND JULIE IT HAD BEEN A PLEASANT, ALMOST leisurely ride back to the Flying V from Camelot. But when they crested the last hill and saw the blackened, still smoldering timbers of what had been the house, Joe had a sudden flashback to a similar scene he had witnessed some years earlier, shortly after the outbreak of the war.

At the war's beginning, neither he nor Win had made a commitment to either side. They didn't own slaves, and they had never owned slaves, so they couldn't see putting their lives on the line to protect the rights of those who did.

On the other hand, they weren't interested in fighting for a federal government against their friends and neighbors. As a result they had managed, for the better part of a year, to stay out of the war.

But that had all changed on the day they returned home from a four-day business trip they had taken on behalf of the family farm.

They had seen smoke rising from the vicinity of their farm, but it hadn't concerned them.

"PA MUST'VE JUST BURNED THE BRUSH. I CAN STILL SEE A little wisp of smoke up there," Win commented. "I thought he was going to wait for us."

"Probably just wanted to show us up," Joe replied. "You know Pa still swears that he can outwork the two of us together."

Win chuckled. "Yeah, well, the hell of it is, I think he can."

They reached the crest of the hill and looked down toward where the house, barn, and other outbuildings should have been. But there were no buildings there. Instead there were several blackened piles of burned-out rubble, all that remained of what had once been the barn, smokehouse, outhouse, and house. Two lonely brick chimneys marked each end of what had been the house and, from the charred skeletal remains, wisps of smoke still curled up into the bright blue sky.

"Joe!" Win shouted. He slapped his heels against the

sides of his horse and it broke quickly into a gallop. Joe did the same with his horse, and they covered the last hundred yards in just a few seconds.

"Ma! Pa!" Win yelled, leaping from his saddle and looking around. Joe was right behind him.

"How'd they let the place catch on fire?" Joe asked.

"It didn't catch on fire," Win answered. "This fire was set."

JOE HAD THAT SAME SICK FEELING NOW THAT HE HAD HAD then. And he had the same certainty that this fire had been set.

"My God! What happened?" Julie asked in a thin, anxious voice. "Our place! It's burned down! Uncle Seth!" she shouted. "Uncle Seth!"

Julie slapped her legs against the sides of the horse she had borrowed from Camelot, urging it into an immediate gallop.

Joe, because he had a bad feeling about what Julie might find, put his horse to gallop as well, trying to head her off. "Julie! No, wait!" he called to her.

Julie was a good horsewoman, well mounted, and considerably lighter than Joe. As a result she reached the ruins of the house several seconds before Joe did, and she was already dismounted and looking through the burned-out rubble by the time Joe arrived.

"Oh, my, look at this, Joe," she moaned. "Look at it. It's gone, all of it." Julie ran her hand through her hair in despair. "I can't imagine how this could've happened." She looked around, her face contorted and on the verge of tears. "And where is Uncle Seth? We have to find him. I must go to him. He needs me now. This . . . this house was his entire life!"

"You wait here," Joe suggested. "I'll look around for him." But seeing that the team Seth had driven was still standing in harness in front of the buckboard, Joe feared the worst.

"No, I'll go with you," Julie said. She shuddered. "And

please, don't say no, I don't think I could stand to be left alone right now.''

Joe nodded, then reached out and put his hand on hers.

''All right,'' he finally said. ''You can come with me. We'll have a look around.''

They found Seth Vincent a few minutes later, lying in a crumpled heap behind the barn where he had been left. Julie began to cry, but she had been prepared for the worst and so finding him this way was not as much of a shock as it could have been.

''Is there anything I can do for you?'' Joe asked. He felt helpless before her sorrow, but he understood it well because he and his brother had found their parents murdered in the ruins of their home.

''Joe, would you put him on the buckboard and take him into town for me, please?'' she asked. ''He was a vestryman in the church, and I think he would like to be buried in the churchyard.'' She looked back toward the burned house, then began crying again. ''Though I have no idea what he will be buried in. He doesn't even have a suit, now that everything has been burned.''

10

JULIE NEEDN'T HAVE WORRIED ABOUT WHAT HER UNCLE Seth would be buried in. He was buried wearing one of the finest suits in Phillip Wellington's wardrobe. Wellington had insisted upon it, just as Pamela had insisted that Julie wear one of her own dresses. With all her things destroyed by the fire, and with no place to go, Julie had no choice but to accept the Wellingtons' generosity, and she did so in the same graciousness with which it was offered. She was taken into their household and treated as if she were a member of the family.

Seth Vincent had been a longtime resident of the valley and was very well liked by all who knew him. As a result the funeral, which was held in Grace Episcopal Church, was attended by all the neighboring ranchers, large and small, as well as by the businessmen of the town. So large was the crowd that the entire service had to be held outside, in the cemetery, in order to accommodate all of the mourners.

The cemetery was typical of all the other graveyards Win had seen. It covered about an acre of land, a cluster of tablets, crosses, and obelisks in wood and stone. Flowers decorated many of the graves. Here and there, small Confederate flags hung limp in the still air while the tombstones by which they stood would proudly proclaim the deceased's service in the "Ninth Texas Cavalry," or "Capp's Company," or "Hardesty's Brigade," ghost units, commanded by specters, in a phantom army.

Win and Joe were standing several yards away from where the burial was taking place. They were under a grove of cottonwood trees, near a large tombstone which had been erected over the grave of a departed Confederate colonel who was one of the specter commanders of that phantom army. They were standing with several of the cowboys, not only from Vincent's ranch and Camelot, but from the neighboring ranches as well. The cowboys were easily separated from the ranchers and businessmen, not only because they were in clean shirts and denim trousers, as opposed to the suits and ties of the ranchers and businessmen, but also because they were men who were obviously uncomfortable in large crowds. They were present for the funeral, but in choosing to stand apart from everyone else they were sharing their private world only with others of their own kind.

Vincent had four hands working for him when he was killed and all four were present for the funeral, not only saddened by the loss of their boss, whom they truly liked, but also anxious as to what their own future would hold now that Seth Vincent was gone. Would the Flying V continue? Would they have jobs?

"You're the one who found Mr. Vincent, aren't you?" one of Vincent's hands said to Joe.

"Yes," Joe answered.

"Is it true that Miss Julie was with you when you found him?"

"Yes."

The cowboy grunted. "Must've been hard on her," he said. "But she's a hardy woman with lots of grit. I reckon she'll get over it, all right." The cowboy stuck out his hand. "My name is Angus. I been workin' for Mr. Vincent ever since I got back from the war."

Joe introduced himself and his brother.

"You didn't see anything unusual around the ranch before it happened, did you, Angus?" Win asked.

Angus shook his head. "Didn't see a thing a'tall. Of

course, me an' the other boys was over to the Double-Diamond at the barbecue they was havin'.''

"Yeah, we know about the barbecue," Joe said. "That's why Mr. Vincent went back home when he did, because he thought someone should be lookin' after the ranch."

"Damn, I'm real sorry to hear that," Angus said. "That makes me feel kinda responsible."

"Why? You had no way of knowing anything like this was going to happen."

"No, I guess not. But I can't help feelin' that way, none-theless. I started not to go, you know. I wish now that I hadn't. Maybe if I'da been there, the two of us coulda run the rustlers off."

"You think that's who it was? Rustlers?" Win asked.

"Well, yeah, it would have to be rustlers, don't you think?" Angus asked. "I mean, from what I hear, they've been workin' the area pretty good. Near 'bout ever'one has lost some cattle to them. The wonder is that Mr. Vincent is the first one to get hisself kilt."

"He ain't the first," one of the other cowboys said. "What about them two boys got themselves kilt in the Black Horse couple of weeks ago?"

"That was different," Angus said. "They wasn't kilt by rustlers. They was kilt by the albino."

"That would be the one they call Shardeen?" Win asked.

"Yeah, Shardeen. That's him, over there, by that wagon. You heard of 'im?"

"No, not till we got here," Win answered. "Some of the boys out at Camelot were talking about him, and about how he shot down a couple of the Cripple C boys in the Black Horse Saloon."

"I hear tell that now, whenever Shardeen goes into the Black Horse, or any other saloon, folks give him all the room he needs," Angus said. "He's a sawed-off runty little bastard, and if it wasn't for them guns, any normal man could break him in two. But there is them guns . . . and that's why Emmerline hired him."

"Joe," Win suddenly said, "have you taken a good look

at Emmerline? Doesn't he look sort of familiar to you?''

Joe looked at Win, then shook his head. "No, I can't say as he does. Somebody looks like that, I don't think I'd forget him.''

"I know it would be sort of hard to forget someone like that," Win agreed. "Still, there's something about him that's nagging at me. I just wish I could put my finger on it.''

AT THE OTHER SIDE OF THE GRAVEYARD, CHAD EMMERline saw Win and Joe Coulter for the first time.

"I'll be damned," he said. "It's the Coulter brothers.''

"What's that?" Shardeen asked.

"Standing over there, with the group of cowboys. Do you see the two men who are apart from the others? One of them is wearing a green shirt, the other a red plaid.''

"Yeah, I see 'em.''

"That's Win and Joe Coulter.''

"Never heard of 'em.''

"You ever heard of Quantrill?''

"Quantrill? Yeah, I've heard of him. He was one of them bushwhackers, wasn't he?''

"He wasn't *one* of the bushwhackers, he was the leader of them," Emmerline said. "And those august gentlemen rode with him. In fact, they were two of his best.''

"You knew them, then?''

"Oh, yes, I knew them. And they knew me, but I was a different person then." Emmerline ran his hand over his bald head, then pulled it down across a face that had been changed and rendered hairless by the explosion. "I was a very different person then.''

"You want me to kill 'em?" Shardeen asked. He asked the question as easily as if he had just inquired if Emmerline wanted him to saddle a horse for him.

"I'll let you know when I want someone killed," Emmerline replied.

"Whatever you say. You're the boss," Shardeen said. He walked over to stand behind the wagon as the funeral continued. He watched the proceedings, or, more specifically, he watched Julie Vincent. He had never seen the woman before today, but he found that he was experiencing a particular erotic joy from knowing that she was the daughter of the man he had killed. That pleasure was enhanced by the fact that he was here, at the funeral of a man he'd killed, watching the grief of that man's daughter.

Shardeen felt himself getting an erection, and he stepped closer so he could use the wagon as a shield and rub himself without being seen. As he fondled himself, he thought of what it would be like with Julie Vincent.

If he could have his way with her, he would tie her up with her arms and legs spread-eagled so that she would be entirely open to him, and defenseless. He would take off all her clothes, and then, as she watched him through terror-filled eyes, he would undress as well.

Julie Vincent would be terrified and that was important, because her fear was a necessary part of his fantasy. Shardeen thought of what it would be like when she found out that she was a prisoner of the same man who had killed her father. She would be both revolted and panic-stricken, and as he considered that reaction, he felt a jolt of pleasure course through him. Because he did not want to shoot off in his pants, he stopped rubbing himself. Then he leaned into the wagon to allow the sensations to subside.

The fantasy continued.

After he informed her that he was the one who'd killed her father, he would then let her know what was in store for her. He longed to see the hot flash of panic she would exhibit when she realized she was going to die.

And how will I kill you, my pretty one? Shardeen asked himself, continuing to coast on the pleasurable sensations. Will I strangle you? Will you die by my knife? Will I shoot you?

In the final analysis, it didn't really matter how she died, as long as she died by his hands . . . and as long as she died with foreknowledge. Her understanding, and the terror that went with that understanding, fueled Shardeen's most exquisite pleasure.

The graveside remarks were concluded at that moment,

and at the invitation of the rector, Julie stepped over to the edge of the open grave and began to spill dirt down onto her uncle's coffin while the priest intoned the committal.

"For as much as it hath pleased Almighty God in His wise providence to take out of this world the soul of our deceased brother Seth, we therefore commit his body to the ground; earth to earth, ashes to ashes, dust to dust."

AFTER THE FUNERAL WELLINGTON ASKED JOE IF HE would drive the buckboard with Pamela and Julie back out to the ranch. Then he asked Win if he would go with him to speak with the barrister.

"To speak to who?"

"The barrister," Wellington repeated. "A solicitor, an attorney. A lawyer," he finally explained, finding the word he was looking for. "I am going to engage him to fight against this scandalous water improvement project."

"A lawyer," Win snorted. "Sure, I'll go with you, but as far as I'm concerned, you're wasting your time."

THE LAW OFFICES OF MORTON, TREGAILIAN, AND GUNN were across the street from the bank. Win and Wellington tied their horses off in front of the office, then went inside, where they were greeted by a rather smallish man in a vested suit and wire-rimmed glasses.

"Lord Wellington," the clerk greeted obsequiously. "How nice to see you."

"Hello, Charles," Wellington returned. "Is Mr. Gunn available?"

"I'll check, sir. I believe he is back from the funeral. Terrible tragedy, Mr. Vincent being killed like that."

"Yes, it was."

A moment later the clerk returned. "Mr. Gunn is in his office," he said. He looked pointedly at Win. "Is this gentleman with you?"

"Yes, and he'll be going in with me," Wellington said.

"Very good, sir. You may go in now," the clerk replied.

Michael Gunn was a large man whose girth strained against the buttons of his vest. A gold watch chain stretched

across the same girth gave the appearance of being added
as a way of reinforcing the overworked buttons. He greeted
Wellington with an extended hand.

"Phillip, my friend," he said. "How nice to see you,
though, admittedly, under sad circumstances." He shook
his head and made a clucking noise. "Poor Seth."

"Yes, it was terrible indeed," Wellington said. He
turned to Win. "Michael, I would like you to meet someone I have recently employed. Mr. Win Coulter."

"Coulter?" Gunn said, screwing up his face. "Might I
have heard that name somewhere?"

"It is possible, Mr. Gunn," Win said without elaborat-
ing.

"Yes, well, what can I do for you, Phillip?" Gunn asked.
Realizing that it was not always healthy to pursue certain
subjects, he let the question of whether or not he knew Win
drop.

"Michael, are you aware of this so-called water improvement project that the federal government has started?"

"Yes, of course I am," Gunn replied. "But what do you
mean, so-called? It was our office that made the application
on behalf of the Valley Cattlemen's Association. Why, you
yourself are a member of that organization. Don't you remember when we discussed it last year? How we wanted
to follow the example you had set by what you did on your
own ranch, and clean out all the channels and streambeds
to provide a better distribution of water throughout the valley."

"Yes, I remember that discussion," Wellington coun-
tered. "But this has nothing to do with that. I'm talking
about the dam that closed off Gypsum River, denying Camelot and every other ranch that depended upon Wolfhole a
source of water. In fact, only the Double-Diamond seems
to have benefited."

"Wait a minute," Gunn said, looking surprised. "You
say a dam was built?"

"Yes."

Gunn walked over to a table and began shuffling through
papers until he found what he was looking for, a map of

the valley. He spread it out on the table, holding the corners down by various makeshift paperweights.

"Now," he said. "Show me where the dam is."

"It's right here," Wellington pointed out. "It is just beyond the boundary lines for Camelot, on public land." Wellington drew his finger down Wolfhole, tracing it across his land, and also following the tributaries that ran from Gypsum River over to adjacent ranches. "And, as you can see, putting a dam here has a disastrous effect on every other piece of property around."

Gunn stroked his chin. "Yes," he said. "Yes, I do see how that could have disastrous effects. I don't know what to tell you, Phillip. This isn't at all what the project was intended to do. If you don't mind, I'm going to have a look into it."

Wellington smiled. "Mind? Michael, that is exactly what I want you to do. That's why I came to you."

11

Pete Barnes, one of the cowboys at Camelot, became so intrigued with Joe's dowsing that he began following him around, watching in curiosity and offering his services when needed. For the first three days after the funeral, Joe continued to explore the grassy meadows of Camelot, without so much as a twitch from his dowsing stick.

After observing him closely for a while, Pete cleared his throat. "Say, Joe, can I try it?" he asked anxiously.

"All right," Joe answered. "But first, you'd better let me show you how it's supposed to work. Now, you see how this here stick is shaped like a wishbone?" he said, holding it out toward him. "What you do is, you hold on to these two arms here. That makes the single arm stick out from the other side, so what you have is an upside-down *Y*."

"Yeah, I know, I know, I been watchin' you," Pete said. "Why don't you let me try it, Joe? I can do it. I know I can do it."

"Sure, if you want to try, go ahead," Joe said. He handed Pete the divining rod, and, almost immediately, the stick pointed down.

"No, you don't want to do that," Joe explained. "You have to keep it out straight."

"Well, I tried to," Pete said, "but soon as I held it out, it just went down by itself."

"Wait a minute, let me see that." Joe took the stick back and held it out over the ground where Pete had been holding it. As it did when it was in Pete's hands, the single arm of the inverted Y pointed straight down. Joe laughed.

"What is it?" Pete asked. "Did I do somethin' wrong?"

"Wrong? No, you did it right. Pete, my boy, you have the gift," Joe said. "I've been looking for water for at least three days, and you find it the first time you touch the stick."

"You mean you think there's water under the ground here?" Pete asked.

"I know there is," Joe replied.

"Well, hell! What are we waitin' for? Let's start digging! I'll get us a couple of shovels," Pete said excitedly as he started back toward the toolshed.

"No, we won't use shovels. There's a better way," Joe answered. "I'll show you."

By noon Win and Joe had rigged a simple water drill. It was the same kind of drilling rig they had used to dig wells on their father's farm, back in Missouri. The drill consisted of three eight-foot poles, formed into a tripod. A pulley was at the apex of the tripod. A rope ran through the pulley, then was tied to a hollow piece of three-inch pipe which hung in perpendicular suspension just beneath the pulley. It was operated by pulling on the rope to lift the pipe, then letting the pipe fall. The weight of the fall would dig up a little of the earth. As it continued to fall, it would dig a hole, bringing in fresh dirt at the bottom of the pipe and pushing out old dirt from the top.

For a while, several people were interested enough in what was going on that the first couple of hours had no end of onlookers, kibitzers, and even a few helpers. By late afternoon, however, with no reward for their attentiveness, most had drifted away to find other tasks to keep them occupied.

Pete, alone, did not lose interest. After all, it was his dowse that had found the sign in the first place, and he was determined to see it through. The result was that, as the long afternoon shadows began to fall across the meadow, only Win, Joe, and Pete were left, sweating in the sun, pulling on the rope and letting the pipe drop, pulling on the rope and letting it drop, pulling it up and letting it drop, over and over again so that by now the hollow pipe was dropping into a narrow hole that was some twenty feet deep.

"Listen to that!" Pete said after one drop.

"What?"

"I heard a gurgle," he said excitedly. "We must've hit water!"

"Drop it in again," Joe ordered, and the pipe was drawn up and dropped again. This time when it was brought up, Joe reached down to the bottom of the pipe, grabbed a handful of the detritus, then began examining it.

"What have you got, Little Brother?" Win asked.

"Mud," Joe replied with a wide grin. He opened his hand to show his find. "We'll be drinkin' water out of here before nightfall."

"Yahoo!" Pete cheered, throwing his hat into the air. "We found it! We found water!"

The cowboys who were close enough to hear the shouting came running out into the field to see what was going on. They brought others, and, when the excitement reached the house, Wellington, Pamela, and Julie came out as well. Even Bascomb, still impeccably dressed in his cutaway jacket, stood by smiling happily at the scene.

" 'Pon my word," Bascomb said quietly. "Who would have ever believed such a thing?"

"How much water do you think there is?" Wellington asked.

"There's a lot of water down there, Mr. Wellington," Joe said. "We can put wells in all over the place. You won't have to worry about water anymore."

"Mr. Coulter, you have my undying gratitude," Wellington said. "You are Moses in the wilderness. You have come to deliver us from the evil of the desert."

"I wish I could take all the credit, Mr. Wellington," Joe

replied. "But the one you should be thanking is Pete. He actually found the water."

"You did?" Wellington asked.

"I reckon I did," Pete replied, beaming. "Joe just give me the stick an' the next thing you know, it was pointin' toward water."

"He has the gift," Joe said. "I wouldn't want to tell you how to run your ranch, but if I was you, I'd make him my full-time water finder. You're goin' to have to have someone around to take care of things after my brother and me are gone."

"Good idea. If you don't mind, Pete, I would like you to stop doing whatever else you have been doing, and help Mr. Coulter find other areas to put in the wells. That will also help you get the experience you will need later on."

"Does that mean I don't have to punch any more cows?" Pete asked. He smiled broadly. "Seein' as how cows is the dumbest critters God ever put on earth, I'd be real happy to quit messin' with them and go to doin' somethin' else! I'm not sure how Cherokee is goin' to take it, though."

"You have my permission to tell Mr. Brown of the new arrangement," Wellington said. "If he has any objections, tell him to come see me."

"Yes, sir!" Pete said happily. "Joe, I'm goin' to go tell Cherokee, then I'll be back to start lookin' for some more wells."

Pete had come under quite a bit of teasing in the last few days for believing in Joe, and even helping him. Now he was completely vindicated as most of the others came around to shake his hand and pat him on the back, congratulating him for being the one to actually find the water.

Pete was enjoying the accolades of all his friends, but the person he had most wanted to know about his participation in finding water was Cherokee. Cherokee had made no bones about the fact that he considered the entire dowsing business to be a waste of time. Once or twice he had even intimated to Pete that if he didn't get back to his regular duties, he would be fired. Now Pete wanted Cherokee to know about his new position. He was working directly for Mr. Wellington himself now. He figured that would mean that Cherokee could no longer hold the threat of firing over Pete's head.

But Pete was frustrated when he saw that Cherokee wasn't in the bunkhouse, corral, or toolshed. He wandered around the place looking for him, and finally wound up in the barn. Standing in the open door at the back of the barn, backlighted by the bright day so that he was in silhouette, Pete saw Gus Thomas. Gus was the ranch farrier, and he was, at that moment, holding a horse's hoof between his knees, filing on the hoof. Gus looked up as Pete approached.

"Well, the hero of the hour," Gus said. He continued to file, and the file made a scraping sound.

"What do you mean?"

Gus knocked the file against a block to clear it, then he blew on it before he resumed the task at hand.

"Well, didn't you find water?"

"Yes," Pete replied. "That is, I helped, but it was mostly Joe Coulter." Pete began looking back into the shadows at the rear of the barn.

"Who are you lookin' for?" Gus asked.

"Well, I was sort of lookin' around for Cherokee," Pete answered. "Ain't been able to find 'im."

Gus chuckled. "Wanna say, 'I told you so,' huh? Well, I can't say as I blame you."

"Yeah, well, not just that. Mr. Wellington, he wants me to search for water full-time. That means I won't be workin' for Cherokee no more."

"I'm sure that breaks your heart," Gus joked.

"You seen 'im around?"

"Yeah, matter of fact, I have. He and Ned rode out of here couple of hours ago, headed south." Using the file, Gus pointed in a southerly direction.

"Thanks," Pete said. "Think I'll ride out and look for him."

"You sure you want to do that? Like as not, he'll be back by nightfall."

"The quicker I tell him, the quicker I can get started in my new job," Pete said as he began saddling a horse. "You say you saw him and Ned headin' south? You got any idea where they was goin'?"

"No," Gus said. He scratched the side of his nose as if in heavy thought, then he smiled. "But Cherokee was ridin' the paint, the one I just shoed the other day. And the right forefoot is carrying a tie-bar shoe. You prob'ly won't have no trouble trackin' 'im down."

"Thanks," Pete said, swinging into the saddle then and heading out toward the south.

As Gus promised, the tie-bar shoe made it easy to pick up their trail, and he was able to keep his horse going at a pretty good clip.

HALF AN HOUR LATER PETE WAS TOTALLY CONFUSED. THE trail had led him into a dead-end canyon and now the trail was gone. It was almost as if Cherokee and Ned had purposely swept the tracks away, as if they didn't want to be followed.

But why would they do something like that?

Pete shook his head, then raised his canteen and took a swallow of water. He recorked the canteen, then wiped his mouth with the back of his hand and looked around.

Where could Cherokee and Ned have disappeared to? The canyon was surrounded on three sides by sheer stone walls, so there was no way out, and no sign to indicate that they had turned around to leave the same way they had entered.

Shaking his head at the mystery of it, Pete hooked his canteen back onto his saddle and started to turn his horse. That was when he heard it. The faint sound of a bawling cow.

Pete stood in the stirrups and looked toward the three walls. Where did that sound come from? There was nothing in here. The walls were solid in front of him, solid to the right of him, solid to left.

He looked toward the wall at the left. Maybe it wasn't quite as solid as the other two walls. It did jut out toward the center somewhat, though he didn't see any opening.

Finally, he decided to ride up to the east wall and have a closer look.

"Damn me!" he said aloud. "I believe there's an opening behind that bulge!"

Urging his horse on, he rode right up to the wall. The bulge, he discovered, wasn't a bulge at all. It was, instead, a needle-shaped rock, set forward from the wall by a few feet. And behind the needle shape there *was* an opening. It was small and could only be seen if someone was right there, and even then they had to be looking for it. But it was there, and it was big enough to allow a horse and rider to get through.

For the first one hundred yards or so Pete thought he had made a mistake coming in here. The path from the opening climbed, sometimes rather sharply, and the floor was so filled with rock that it made the footing quite treacherous.

But he rode on, driven now as much by curiosity as by any need to find Cherokee. The echoes of his horse's footfalls rolled up and down the high-walled fissure as if they were rolling timpani.

Ahead of him, and even above the sound of his horse's hoofbeats, he could hear the rattle of rock upon rock. The noise grew loud and urgent, and by the time Pete figured out what it was, he just barely managed to pull up in time to avoid the fall of several fist-size rocks. He didn't know what had caused them to fall, but from the amount of rock and stone on the ground, it was obviously a frequent occurrence.

Pete was about to turn around and go back when, once more, he heard the sound of a bawling cow. And this time there was no mistaking where it came from. It was coming from straight ahead!

Now he was nearly consumed with curiosity. Why did the hoofprints disappear? Where did this hidden trail lead to? And what was the source of the cow sounds he was hearing?

The passageway became even more narrow until Pete could reach out and touch either side. Then the path quit climbing. It continued on an even level for the better part of fifty yards, then it started going back down. And, as it went down, it widened until finally it was a broad, easily negotiated path. Then ahead, just beyond a large boulder, Pete saw an open field.

"I'll be damned!" he said aloud. He slapped his legs against the sides of his horse, putting it into a canter. When he reached the flat field, he saw hundreds of cattle milling about in this, a natural corral.

What were these cows doing here? Where did they come from?

Looking around further, Pete saw that there was a branding operation in progress.

"What the hell?" Pete mused aloud. "What would they be brandin' at this time of year? Besides which, them cows is full-growed."

By now consumed with curiosity, Pete started toward the group he saw doing the branding. Most of the men were strangers to him, but he recognized Cherokee and Ned.

"What the hell! Who are you?" one of the strange cowboys asked when he looked up and saw Pete upon them. Hearing the cowboy's exclamation of surprise, Cherokee turned around. When he saw Pete, his eyes opened wide.

"Pete, what the hell are you doing here?" Cherokee asked.

It took Pete only a moment to realize what was going on. Cherokee, Ned, and the other men weren't branding cows, they were making adjustments on a brand that had already been burned into the cows' hides. The brand that was there was the *W*. Cherokee was using another *W* branding iron, but this time he was inverting it, closing the top of the existing brand with his new brand so that the end result was two diamonds. The Double-Diamond.

"My God!" Pete said. "Cherokee, what are you doin' with these men? They're rustlin' Camelot cattle!"

Pete turned his horse around and started back toward the opening at full gallop.

"Don't let the son of a bitch get away!" Cherokee

shouted, and he and the others with him pulled their guns and began blazing away.

Primer caps snapped and charges exploded as the robbers began banging away at Pete. Pete bent low over the horse's withers, urging him to go faster. A bullet carried off his hat, another whistled by his ear, and he saw still others kicking up dirt and chipping rock in front of him.

For a moment it looked as if Pete might make it. Then a bullet crashed into the back of his head and he tumbled off his horse, dead before he hit the ground.

The horse, panicked by the shooting, continued at a gallop, even faster now without its rider. With empty stirrups slapping against its flanks, it ran back through the pass, then headed toward the ranch.

"SEE IFFEN YOU CAN KNOCK THAT LEANER PLUMB OFFEN there, Eb," one of the cowboys called.

Eb Peters spit in his hands and rubbed them together, then held the horseshoe in front of his eyes, sighting on the stake at the far pit.

"He's goin' to do it," one of the watching cowboys said.

"The hell he is. I'll tell you what he's goin' to do. What he's goin' to do is knock that there horseshoe right down onto the stake an' I'm goin' to have me another ringer," Gus boasted.

Gus was generally known as the best horseshoe thrower on the ranch, but a young cowboy named Eb was having a particularly good day today and was giving the champion a run for his money.

"Come on, Eb, you can do it," somone called. "I got a quarter ridin' on you!"

"Careful, Eb, careful," somone else urged.

Eb rocked back and forth, then swung his arm forward, tossing the shoe. It knocked Gus's leaner away, hooked onto the top of the stake, spun around three times, then dropped with a satisfying clang as a ringer. The toss guaranteed the win, and everyone cheered Eb, not because Gus was unpopular, but because Gus was so seldom beaten.

Gus, with a wide grin, was the first one to congratulate Eb.

"Well," he teased, "I guess I must've taught you too well."

At that very moment a saddled but riderless horse came trotting up.

"Hey, look at that!" someone called.

"Where'd that horse come from?"

"Ain't that the horse Pete was ridin'?"

A couple of cowboys ran out in front of the horse and held their hands out toward the tired but still skittish animal. With shushing sounds they calmed it, then reached out and grabbed the reins.

"This is Pete's horse," one of the cowboys said. "I recognize his saddle."

"Shit, Arnie, look here," the other cowboy who had helped catch the horse said. He was standing on the opposite side.

"What?"

"Here, on the saddle. This here is blood, ain't it?"

12

EB SAID HE THOUGHT PETE HAD A BROTHER BACK IN AR-kansas, but he wasn't sure. Gus said it might have been a cousin. It wasn't until the funeral when Buford Coleman, one of the four men who had worked on the Flying V before Vincent was killed, cleared it up for them.

"Me an' Pete come out here from Mississippi together," he said. "He's got a sister back in Iuka, but they don't get along any too good. She married a Yankee carpetbagger, and Pete wouldn't have nothin' to do with him, or her either."

"Hell, who could blame him for that?" Eb said. "Ain't bad enough those Yankee bastards come down here an' take all our land, they got to take our women too."

"What are we goin' to do with Pete's things?" Gus asked.

"Mr. Coleman, you knew Pete longer than anyone else?" Wellington asked.

"Yes, sir, I reckon I did."

"Then I shall give his saddle to you," Wellington said. "I believe that is his most valuable possession."

Buford grinned. "Why, I thank you, Mr. Wellington. That's plumb decent of you."

"The rest of you men, draw lots for what is left. That seems to be the only fair thing," Wellington continued.

Neither Win nor Joe had put their names in the pot, so they were able to watch the drawing dispassionately. Cherokee, because he was the foreman, was also out of the drawing, and was standing to one side watching the proceedings. Win ambled over to talk to him.

"Mr. Wellington said you and Ned are the ones who brought Pete in," Win said.

"That's right," Cherokee replied.

"Where'd you find him?"

"Up north, near the breaks."

"You sure about that?"

Cherokee glared at Win. "Some reason I ought not to be sure?" he asked.

"No, not really, I suppose," Win said. "But his horse came in from the south."

"What the hell does that mean?" Cherokee growled. "Horses is dumb as dirt. He probably wandered around out on the range for a while until he found the place, that's all."

"Yeah, that could be," Win agreed. "Though horses usually come back home in a straight line. 'Specially if they're somewhat skittish, like that one was."

"Look, I don't know nothin' about his horse," Cherokee said. "All I know is where Ned and me found the body. It was up by the breaks."

"If you say so," Win said. "Although, it does seem a little odd that he left here heading south, and his horse came back in from the south."

"Look, I don't know what you're tryin' to make out of all this," Cherokee said. "And, anyhow, what business is it of yours?"

"None, I reckon."

"That's what I figured," Cherokee said with a dismissive snort.

"CHEROKEE SAYS THEY FOUND HIM UP NORTH," WIN SAID to Joe that night as the two brothers discussed the situation in their little room behind the tack room.

"Yeah, I heard he was saying that," Joe said. "But Gus

swears he saw Pete ridin' south to look for Cherokee.''

''Yeah, and south is where Cherokee has been goin' just about every day,'' Win said.

''Which means the son of a bitch is lyin' when he says he found Pete up by the breaks.''

''That's right,'' Win said.

''You think Cherokee killed Pete?'' Joe asked, studying Win through hooded eyes.

''Yeah, I think he did,'' Win answered without hesitation.

''The only question is, why did he kill him? What would he stand to gain?'' Joe asked.

''Don't forget, Cherokee and Ned have been leaving out of here every day, going south with a branding iron in their saddlebag. I think Pete happened onto them while they were doing something they shouldn't have been doing . . . like perhaps changing the brands.''

''You mean you think Cherokee's stealing cows? From Mr. Wellington?'' Joe asked.

Win nodded. ''He's stealin' cows bigger'n shit. And my guess is, poor old Pete must've stumbled onto them. When he threatened to tell, Cherokee or Ned shot him.''

''Yeah, well, whoever did it did more than just shoot him. He had half a dozen bullet holes in him,'' Joe said.

At that precise moment, they both heard a sound, the quiet step of someone approaching. Both men drew their guns and pointed them toward the door of their room.

The step was bolder, then someone knocked on the door.

''Joe?'' a woman called. They recognized the voice as belonging to Julie.

The brothers smiled and put their pistols away, then Joe walked over to open the door. Julie was standing nervously, just on the other side of the door.

''I hope my visit isn't unwelcome,'' Julie said. ''For if it is, kindly tell me, and I'll leave.''

''No, it's not unwelcome at all,'' Joe said, stepping back to invite her in. ''In fact, you are very welcome. Isn't that right, Win?''

"Yes, of course, beautiful women are always welcome," Win answered.

"Uh, thank you," Julie said, clearing her throat. "You are most gracious."

"Yes, well, it's too bad Win won't be able to stay and visit with us," Joe went on, hinting broadly. "But he was just telling me how he needed to go out and check on all the well sites."

For a moment Win didn't know what Joe was talking about, then he caught on and grinned broadly. "That's right," he said, reaching for his hat. "I need to check them over . . . all of them, the ones we've already dug and the ones we haven't yet started."

"Take your time, Win. You remember what Pa always used to say. A thing's not worth doin', unless you take the time to do it right."

"I remember," Win said. "Good night, Miss Vincent," he added, putting on his hat.

Joe stood at the door until his brother was gone, then he turned back toward Julie. The smile on her face told Joe that she hadn't been fooled for one moment. She knew exactly why Win had left them alone. What's more, the smile told Joe that she approved of the ploy.

"I would offer you something to drink," Joe said, "but I don't have anything."

"Who needs anything to drink?" Julie asked. Raising her arms, she took two steps toward Joe. A moment later her body was plastered against his, while her arms went around him, pulling him to her.

"You sure you want to do this?" Joe asked. He reached up to let his hand rest lightly on her neck.

"Want to do this?" Julie replied in a husky voice. "Joe Coulter, I don't think *want* has anything to do with it. I have to do it. I've been able to think of nothing else, from the moment I first saw you. It's frightening to me. I want to run away, yet here I am, and I don't know why. Can you tell me why?"

"Maybe it's because you've never had a man, and you're wonderin' what it's like," Joe suggested. "Or, maybe you have had a man, and you remember how good it was and you want to do it again. I don't know which it is, and I don't care to know which it is. All that's important to me is that you are here now.''

''But it is foolish, isn't it?'' Julie asked. ''I mean, you do agree with me that this is a very foolish thing for me to do?''

''I don't agree at all,'' Joe said. ''You're a woman full growed, and I'm a man. I figure whatever we do between us is . . . well . . . between us.''

''And what, exactly, are we going to do?'' Julie asked in a breathless voice.

''You *know* what we're going to do,'' Joe answered. He unbuttoned his trousers and slid his pants down. By now he was totally erect, and when it sprang up, she reacted in an audible gasp.

Joe put his hand up behind her head and pulled her mouth to his. He kissed her lightly at first, then harder as he felt her hand move boldly to the shaft of his penis.

Joe began to undo the buttons on Julie's dress. With her free hand she helped unfasten the bodice. The combination of light from the kerosene lantern and the silver moon played across her flesh, disclosing large, firm breasts and nipples which were pink and erect with desire.

Julie slipped the garment from her body, then stood naked in the soft light. Her smooth flesh gleamed. Her legs were shapely and strong, and met at a luxurious growth of red hair. He held his arms out to her, and she went into them, kissing him deeply, pressing her naked flesh against his, pushing her hard little nipples into his chest. Her fingers raked down his back, across his buttocks, teased the crack of his ass, then closed on his scrotum.

Joe moved lower with his mouth, along her jawline to her ear, where he made her gasp by sticking his tongue inside her. He trailed his tongue down her throat to her shoulder, then across the soft, smooth flesh of her breast to touch it to the nipple. He took it between his teeth and chewed on it ever so gently, then he began to suck.

''Oh, yes,'' Julie breathed. ''This is what I want. This is

what I've been dreaming about!'' Her hand grasped his cock, squeezed it, then worked up and down the shaft.

She kissed his forehead, then his hair. Then, as effortlessly as if he were picking up a child, Joe swept her up and carried her over to deposit her on his bunk. A moment later he was on the bed beside her, then over her, as she offered herself to him. She guided him into her.

Joe withheld his thrust for a moment to kiss her again. Then he stuck his tongue into her mouth at the same time he pushed himself into her velvet cleft. She let out a little whimper, but thrust her hips up as hard as she could, taking him into her hot, pulsing tunnel.

Julie flailed about wildly beneath him, gyrating her hips, forcing him to stay with her, to ride her like a bucking bronco. He thrust all the way in, then pulled out, then rammed it home again while she squeezed him with tiny but intense muscle spasms.

''Oh . . . oh . . . I feel so . . .'' she said as her feelings began approaching a crescendo. Then she cried out in sharp little moans as she crashed over the peak of her first orgasm, then moved quickly in search of another. Lightning struck her a second time, then a third, and she shuddered with the pleasure of it.

Joe stayed with her. The fire in her body spread to his until finally he could hold it back no longer. He felt the sweet hot boiling of his own blood and sperm as he shot his seed deep inside her.

JOE HEARD SOMEONE OUTSIDE, IN THE DARKNESS, COMING in from riding nighthawk, the horse's hoofbeats ringing hollowly. From over in the bunkhouse he heard a man's low, rumbling voice, followed by the laughter of several of the cowboys. Out on the prairie he heard a coyote howl.

''Oh,'' Julie said quietly. ''For me to come out here like this. What you must think of me.''

''I think you are quite a lady,'' Joe said.

''You must believe me,'' she said. ''I've never done anything like this before.''

''I know.''

"I'm telling the truth. I've never—"

"It don't matter," Joe said, interrupting her gently. "Remember?"

"Oh . . . oh, yes, I suppose you're right," she said.

She had been lying beside him, but she got up now and walked over to the back window to look out onto the ranch. He could see her clearly in the soft, golden light of the lantern and the silver glow of the moon. Her breasts were in bold relief, her nipples erect, but the lower part of her body was shrouded in shadow.

"See anything?" Joe asked. The window looked away from the bunkhouse, out over the prairie.

"Just the moon," she said. She began putting her clothes on then, and she chuckled softly.

"What is it?" Joe asked.

"Promise you won't laugh?"

"I promise."

"From now on, every time I look at the moon in this phase, I'm going to remember this night, and it's going to make me very . . . what is it you men say? Randy?"

Joe raised up on one elbow and looked at her. "Is that a fact?" he said.

"That is a fact, Joe Coulter," she answered. She pulled on her bloomers. "And whoever I am with at the time is going to get quite a surprise," she added with a challenging smile.

"Why is that?"

"Because I am going to throw myself at him, and the whole time he is taking me . . . I am going to be thinking of you."

13

WIN WAS ABSOLUTELY POSITIVE THAT CHEROKEE WAS rustling Camelot cattle. He was going to suggest as much to Wellington, but every time he mentioned Cherokee's name, Wellington would make some comment as to how lucky he was to have found a man like Cherokee to run his ranch for him. It therefore became obvious to Win that before he accused Cherokee, he was going to have to have some proof.

It was to obtain that proof that Win and Joe decided to spend a few nights out on the range just to keep an eye on things. They told no one of their plans, not Wellington, neither of the women, and none of the cowboys, since they didn't know who among the cowboys would be loyal to Cherokee and who would be loyal to the man who actually paid their wages.

Win and Joe rode out onto the range early in the afternoon, and when it grew dark, they took up a position that would enable them to keep an eye on the herd, or at least as much of the herd as the moonlight would show. They built a campfire, then let it burn down until the flickering flames were gone so that there remained only the red and orange gleam of the embers. An open can of beans sat on a flat rock Win had put inside the glowing coals, and a small wisp of steam curled from the top. Win and Joe sat near the fire waiting for the beans to warm. Win leaned over to look into the can.

"Looks like it's about ready," he said. "We'll cut up a pepper or two and it'll be a fine meal."

"It's a hell of a long way from being a meal, no matter what you do to it," Joe snarled.

"Joe, I swear, boy, you'd bitch if you was hung with a new rope," Win chortled.

Out in the darkness a calf, separated from the others by a casual shifting of the herd, bawled in fright, to be answered by the reassuring call of its equally anxious mother.

"Did you bring any peaches?" Joe asked hopefully. Both brothers had a fondness for canned peaches and, whenever they could, kept one or two tins of the fruit in their saddlebags.

"We ate the last of the peaches, remember?" Win answered. He tasted a spoonful of beans. "Oh, I love 'em," he said. "They're great."

Joe held out his tin plate, and Win spooned half the can onto it. Joe took a mouthful, then made a face.

"You love 'em, you say? I'll tell you one thing, Big Brother, if you ever get hitched up, your wife's goin' to have an easy row to hoe to please you, 'cause if you love this, it sure as shit don't take much."

"Hitched? Now how the hell can I ever get hitched?" Win teased. "Seems to me like I've took you to raise."

Both men heard it at the same time. It was a quiet sound, a subtle sound which the average person might never have discerned, but which stood out sharply to senses which, over the war years and in the time since, had been finely honed to discern potential danger. The sound they heard was horse's hooves, as distinguished from the clatter of the hooves of thousands of milling cattle.

"Someone's comin' around," Joe hissed.

"Yeah, I hear," Win replied. Both plates of beans were set down as the men moved quickly toward their rifles.

Win made a silent motion with his hand to send Joe around one side, while he started around the other. They moved stealthily through the night, toward the sound of the intruder.

When Win reached an open area, he ran through the night, crouched low, keeping an eye on the ground before him in the dim moonlight so he wouldn't trip. Off to his right was a large mass of cattle, the herd he and Joe were watching. Beyond the herd the horizon was blocked out by the large, dark mass of a nearby mesa. That made it impossible to see in silhouette anyone who might be sneaking around.

Win followed the meandering Frog Creek up to a higher elevation. It was Frog Creek and its meager source of water that had sustained the herd since Gypsum River was dammed. Win couldn't help but notice how little water remained in Frog Creek now, which made the wells he and Joe were digging all the more important. Within a month, Frog Creek would be dry and the wells would be the only source of water. But with two wells in and a third begun, Win felt certain they would be equal to the task.

Win reached a rock outcropping about three quarters of the way up the draw, and he lay flat on it and looked out over the herd. It was difficult to see anything more than a large, black mass.

"Win!" Joe yelled. "I see two men over toward the butte!"

A flash of fire and a rifle shot followed Joe's call, and Win knew that he had fired on the men.

The rifle shot startled the two horsemen into activity and they both left at a gallop. Their sudden movement and the sound of their horses alerted Win to their presence, and he too fired at them, not really trying to hit either of them, but merely trying to spur their retreat on.

"Yaaheeeeeehah!" Joe screamed, giving the Rebel yell. "Look at them sons of bitches skedaddle!"

Win hurried back down the creek bank until he returned to their campsite. He had gone farther than Joe, so Joe was already there by the time he returned.

"Who do you think that was?" Joe asked. He was still pumped up with the excitement of the encounter, and his smile and wide eyes told Win he was enjoying this more than digging wells. "You think it was Cherokee?"

"No, I don't think so," Win answered. "I just got a glimpse of 'em. I didn't see them clear, but neither one of them sat their saddle the way Cherokee or Ned does."

"Yeah, well, maybe it wasn't Cherokee or Ned, but I'll bet it was cattle rustlers. They prob'ly thought that over on this side there wouldn't be anyone watchin' over the herd."

"The reason they thought that was because they were probably told that," Win said. "By Cherokee," he added.

"What was that?" someone's voice called from the night.

"Anybody see anything?" another voice asked.

"Listen, boys, we better split up and ride around the herd," another said. "Like as not, they're real skittish about now."

Win started putting out their campfire. "Gather up your gear, Joe," he hissed. "Let's move back out of the way until they get the herd quiet again. I'd just as soon not be seen out here. I don't want to answer any questions."

"Good idea," Joe agreed.

WIN AND JOE MOVED THEIR CAMP FAR ENOUGH AWAY from the edge of the herd to avoid being discovered by any of the night-riding cowboys, and there they spent the night. The next morning the first pink fingers of dawn touched the sagebrush, and the light was soft and the air was cool. Win liked the range best early in the morning. He liked the way the last morning star made a bright pinpoint of light over the purple range mountains which lay in a ragged line far to the west.

Win got a fire going, then threw chunks of mesquite wood onto it, stirring the fire into crackling flames which danced merrily against the bottom of the suspended coffee-pot. A rustle of wind through feathers caused him to look up just in time to see a golden eagle diving on its prey. The eagle swooped back into the air carrying a tiny desert mouse which kicked fearfully in the eagle's claws. A rabbit bounded quickly into its hole, frightened by the sudden appearance of the eagle.

Win poured himself a cup of coffee and sat down to enjoy it. It was black and steaming, and he had to blow on it before he could suck it through his extended lips. He watched the sun peak above the nearby mesa, then stream brightly down onto the open range.

Joe had gone out a short time ago to take a look around. Now he came back in.

"Uhm, uhm, that coffee smells awful good," Joe said, swinging down from his saddle and walking toward the fire, rubbing his hands together in eager anticipation. "I wouldn't mind havin' a biscuit and some bacon, either."

"I've got some jerky in my saddlebag if you'd care for any," Win said.

"No, thanks," Joe replied. "I reckon I've et enough range candy when I had to. I ain't so hungry now that I can't wait till we get back to the cookhouse where we can get us a real breakfast."

"Can't say as I blame you," Win said.

Joe poured himself a cup of coffee, and as Win had before him, blew on it, sucking it noisily through his lips.

"Win, I seen somethin' strange out there," Joe said.

"Strange? What do you mean, strange?"

"Out there, by the washout, I found tracks goin' into the herd."

"Into the herd?"

"Yeah. It's like, instead of comin' to steal cattle, they was here to bring some back. Now, why would they do that, do you reckon?"

"Maybe it was goin' to be like a Judas goat," Win suggested. "You know, bring a lead steer in, have him mix with the herd, then cut away, bringin' several cows with it. That's what they sometimes do in a slaughterhouse."

"Could be," Joe said. He chuckled. "Onliest thing is, this here steer now belongs to Camelot."

"Yeah. We probably not only saved Wellington's cows,

we saved the other ranchers' cows as well. Even ole Emmerline ought to thank us.''

"Emmerline," Joe snorted. "Hell, it wouldn't surprise
me none if that son of a bitch wasn't behind it, the way he
tried to cheat all the other cattlemen out of their water.''

Win tossed the final dregs of his coffee into the fire.
"Well, what do you say we get on back to the ranch? If
we start now we'll be back in time for breakfast, and no
one will ever know we spent the night out here.''

THE NEAREST TOWN TO CAMELOT RANCH WAS LORAINE,
Texas, and in his office in Loraine, a nervous Harper Canby
examined the letter that had arrived with the morning post.

UNITED STATES DEPARTMENT
OF THE INTERIOR
WASHINGTON, D.C.
August 23, 1870

The Honorable Harper Canby
Commissioner, Water Resources
Loraine, Texas

Dear Mr. Canby,

This department is in receipt of a letter, dated the
3rd, instant, in which the writer, Mr. Michael Gunn, a
lawyer in Loraine, Texas, raises the claim that the water improvement project in your charge has deprived
several ranchers of the water which normally flows
across their land.

You are directed to visit Mr. Gunn and the ranchers
who have raised the claim and explain that the clearing
out of canals and channels will increase, and not de-
crease the flow of water. You will also assure him that
there are no plans for a dam, as he has expressed some
concern about an alleged dam across Gypsum River.

An inspector will be in your area one month from

now, and he will help you explain the project to those who are apprehensive about it. Your Obedient Servant,

Columbus Delano
Secretary of the Interior

Canby put the letter to one side, then poured himself a stiff drink. What was he going to do when the inspector arrived? There was no dam authorized, and yet the dam at Gypsum River was most obviously there.

Emmerline, he thought. It was Emmerline who'd persuaded him to build the dam in the first place. It was Emmerline who'd convinced him that in the long run the dam was better for the ranchers because it would preserve the water. It was Emmerline who had said he would guarantee that there would be no trouble as a result of building the dam, and it was Emmerline who'd furnished the "deputies" who stood guard while the dam was being built, one of whom had nearly caused a catastrophe by attacking Phillip Wellington. Fortunately, Wellington had survived and there were no repercussions . . . but if the blow had been a little more severe, the result could have been disastrous.

The situation was becoming untenable and Canby was going to have to find some way out. And, as far as he was concerned, the person to show him the way out would have to be Chad Emmerline.

Canby had sent for Emmerline as soon as he received the letter from the Secretary of the Interior and was now waiting for him. The messenger had returned with the news that Emmerline would be by to see him at four o'clock, and it was nearly that now.

Canby poured himself a second drink and was just lifting it to his lips when the door to his office opened and Emmerline came in.

"See here, Canby," Emmerline said angrily. "How dare you send a messenger to me, demanding that I come see you? There is enough talk about my profiting from the water project as it is. If it gets out that you and I are in collusion, the situation can get much worse."

How like a grub-worm he looks, Canby thought, studying the round, hairless head of the man in front of him. Canby took his drink, without answering Emmerline's outburst.

"Well, you sent for me," Emmerline said when Canby didn't reply. "What is it? What is the problem?"

"What is the problem? I'll tell you what the problem is," Canby answered. He pointed to the letter. "I just got a letter from Mr. Columbus Delano. You do know who he is, don't you? He is the Secretary of the Interior. And he is sending an inspector out here next month."

"So?"

"So? So?" Canby answered, so agitated now that his voice trilled up into falsetto. "What do you suppose is going to happen when the inspector discovers a dam where no dam has been authorized?"

"Give him the same story you've been giving the ranchers," Emmerline said easily. "Just tell him that you had to dam Gypsum River off because it was diverting too much water from the Colorado River."

"He won't believe that."

"He'll have to believe it," Emmerline said. "It will be up to you to convince him."

"That's just it," Canby said. "I'm afraid! If he starts asking me questions, I don't know if I can handle it."

"Don't be such a nervous Nellie and you'll handle it just fine," Emmerline said. Emmerline smiled and took out his pipe, then, very slowly and deliberately, began tamping the bowl. It was as if, by that action, he was able to calm the fears of Canby, and he took a few seconds attending to his task before he spoke again. And when he did speak, he spoke in a measured, calm voice.

"After all," he said, lighting his pipe and taking audible puffs in between words. "The only real troublemaker around here is Mr. Wellington. And I have a feeling that we won't be having any more problems with him. Very soon now, he's going to have more trouble than he can handle, and he's not going to have time to worry about the dam, water rights, or anything else."

"What are you talking about?" Canby asked. "What kind of trouble?"

Emmerline clenched the mouthpiece of the pipe in his teeth and smoke encircled his head as he answered Canby's question.

"The very worst kind of trouble a cattleman can have," Canby said mysteriously. "And if I were you, I wouldn't want to know any more about it."

"I don't, I don't," Canby said, holding up his hands. "But, Mr. Emmerline, what are we going to do about this?" He pointed to the letter.

"I can't be bothered with that right now," Emmerline answered. "When the time comes, I'm certain you will handle it."

"But I was counting on you for that, Mr. Emmerline. I went way out on a limb for you, and I'm counting on your help."

Emmerline stood up to leave Canby's office, but before he left, he looked back at Canby and pointed at him with his pipe. "Canby, when it gets right down to it, I've already paid you for your services. A little sum of ten thousand dollars, I believe, for which you were so gracious as to sign a receipt."

"Oh, my God, the receipt!" Canby said, putting his hand over his mouth. "I had forgotten that you made me sign that foolish thing. Please, you mustn't ever let anyone see that! That could put me in prison!"

"Yes, it could, couldn't it?" Emmerline said blandly. "I should think that would be enough incentive to ensure that the government inspectors cause us no problems. Now, you find a way to handle it yourself, Canby, and quit crying to me. I'm out of this deal entirely. I bought myself out when I paid you the money." Emmerline smiled. "Good day, Canby."

14

IT WAS THE MIDDLE OF THE NIGHT WHEN WIN HEARD THE conversation taking place in the corral. He fought against the intrusion into his sleep, but the persistent voices continued.

"All I'm askin' is that you ride out with me an' take a look," Eb was saying. "I'm tellin' you, there's somethin' wrong."

"It's four o'clock in the mornin'," Cherokee's voice replied gruffly. "I ain't ridin' out at four o'clock in the mornin', just 'cause one of the nighthawks has found a few sick cows."

"Win?" Joe's voice came from the dark. "Win, you awake?"

"Yeah," Win answered. "I am now."

"What do you think is going on?"

"I don't know, but I'm going to find out." Win pulled on his pants, then his boots.

"Yeah, wait a minute, I'm goin' with you," Joe said.

The two men dressed very quickly, then stepped outside to join the two men who were having the conversation. Cherokee was in his long johns, as if just rousted from his bed. Eb, who was fully dressed, was standing in front of his horse, holding the reins.

"What's goin' on?" Win asked. "What are you doing

in here, Eb? I thought you were ridin' nighthawk tonight."

"I am," Eb answered. "That is, I was, till I saw somethin' I thought Cherokee might want to take a look at. But he don't seem none too interested," he added with a derisive look at the foreman.

"You want somebody to go look at the cows with you, take these two," Cherokee said, taking in Win and Joe with a wave of his hand. "They're the ones Wellington has hired to take care of trouble. And it seems to me like what you're talkin' about is trouble."

"You're mighty damn right. If it's what I think it is, it could be big trouble," Eb said. "And bein' as you're the foreman, it seems to me that, by rights, you should be the one goin' out to see about it. Either you or Mr. Wellington."

"No matter what it is, there ain't nothin' I could do about it at this time of night. And whatever it is you found, or you think you found, will still be there come daylight. I'll take a look at it then," Cherokee said. He started back toward the bunkhouse, from which could be heard the sound of a dozen or more snoring sleepers.

"I'll be damned," Eb said as Cherokee walked away. "Never thought I'd see him do anything like that."

"What is the problem, Eb?" Win asked.

"Is it true, what Cherokee said? Are you two boys lookin' out for trouble for Mr. Wellington?"

"I reckon you could say that," Joe answered.

"Well, I don't know as there's anything you can do about this bit of trouble," Eb said. "But the boss needs to know about it, and since Cherokee won't come take a look at it, maybe you boys will."

"Sure, we'll ride out with you," Win said.

They didn't speak during the ride. Eb was a man of few words, and Win knew that he preferred to show him the problem, whatever it was, rather than tell him about it.

Finally, after a ride of some six or seven miles, and with a faint light beginning to crack in the east, they reached a small herd of no more than a hundred or so cows.

"What is it?" Win asked. "What did you want to show me?"

Eb sat in his saddle, looking out over the small herd. Then he saw what he was looking for, and, without a word, he pointed.

Win and Joe saw the cow Eb was pointing to. It was drooling from the mouth, and as it walked it would draw up first one foot, then the other.

"What is that?" Win asked. "What's wrong with that cow?" The two brothers dismounted and walked over toward the animal.

"I think I can tell you," Joe said. He kneeled beside the cow and looked at its hooves. On the skin, just above the hooves, there were dozens of blisters.

"Oh, shit! Look at this, Win," Joe said, pointing to the right forefoot.

"What is it, Joe?" Win asked. "You know more about these critters than I do."

"I hope I'm wrong, but it looks to me like this cow has hoof-and-mouth disease," Joe answered, standing up and brushing his hands on his pants.

"Yeah, that's what I thought it was too," Eb said. The young cowboy was still mounted. "I told Cherokee, but he didn't seem none too surprised about it."

"What?" Win asked.

"I said I told Cherokee, but he didn't seem none too worried about it. Leastwise, he wasn't worried enough to come out here and check it out."

"That's not what you said," Win said. "You said he didn't seem too surprised."

"Yeah, well, that too, I guess," Eb said. "I mean, well, when I told him he just sort of shrugged his shoulders like as if he was sayin', 'So what?' "

"This hoof-and-mouth disease," Win said. "Is it pretty bad?"

"Bad? I'll say it's bad," Eb said. "It's bad enough that the entire herd will have to be destroyed, and then buried in quicklime."

"You mean all these cows?" Win asked.

"No, sir, I mean ever' cow Mr. Wellington's got on the place. That's the law."

"Surely there is no call to do all that?" Win asked.

"Yeah, I'm afraid there is," Joe replied with a sigh. "Soon as word gets out about this, Mr. Wellington won't have no choice. He'll be forced to do it."

"Then, there's no need for word of this to ever get out, is there?" Win suggested. "All we have to do is kill that one cow."

"I don't know, Big Brother, that's awful dangerous," Joe protested. "Hoof-and-mouth disease is a bad thing, and if it gets out, it could wipe out ever' cow in this part of the state. I'd hate to think we was responsible for that."

"I know, but . . ." Win stopped in mid-sentence, then took a closer look at the infected animal. "I'll be damned. This isn't even one of Mr. Wellington's beeves."

"What do you mean, he ain't one of our'n?" Eb asked in surprise.

"Look at the brand," Win suggested, pointing to the animal's rump. "What brand is that? It sure isn't Mr. Wellington's."

Eb dismounted and walked over to look at the brand. Instead of the familiar *W*, he saw an *S* sitting over a section of a circle, the ends curving upward.

"A Rocking S," Eb said.

"Is the Rocking S nearby?" Win asked.

Eb shook his head. "Not that I know of, and I know prob'ly ever' ranch within a hundred miles in any direction. Never heard of this one."

"How did a cow from a ranch that's nowhere around here get here?" Win asked.

"And a diseased one at that," Joe added.

Win snapped his fingers. "Son of a bitch," he said. "Joe, I know where this cow come from."

"Shit, I think I do too," Joe said. "It was the other night, wasn't it?"

Win nodded his head. "Yes. It wasn't rustlers we spooked. We thought we scared them away, but they didn't come to steal any cows. They did exactly what they intended to do, and that is put this cow into the herd.''

''What are you two boys talkin' about?'' Eb asked.

Quickly, Win explained how he and Joe had spent the night watching the herd a few days before. He told him, also, about seeing a couple of riders, then running them off.

''We thought they was tryin' to put a leadin' steer into the herd to take some cows off with it,'' Joe said. ''But they ain't one bit of doubt in my mind but that them two riders, whoever they was, left this cow.''

''My God, who would do somethin' like that?'' Eb asked. ''Don't they know they could infect the entire herd?''

Win nodded. ''They not only knew it,'' he said, ''that's *why* they done it.''

''Emmerline,'' Joe snorted.

''That would be my guess,'' Win said.

''Hold on there,'' Eb said. ''Mr. Emmerline, he's got cows of his own. Why would he want to go and affect an entire herd?''

''Because he wants Camelot,'' Win replied. ''And he figures that if he wipes out Wellington's herd, Wellington won't be able to go on.''

''What pisses me off is the son of a bitch is going to get away with it,'' Joe snarled.

''Maybe not,'' Win replied.

''Win, we've got no choice,'' Joe said. ''Mr. Wellington's herd is going to have to be destroyed.''

''I agree with you as far as these animals are concerned,'' Win said. ''They have been exposed and they are going to have to be killed. But we may be able to save the rest of the herd.''

''How?'' Joe asked. ''And how are we going to kill this many cows without arousing some suspicion?''

Win shook his head. ''I'm afraid I don't have an answer to that question.''

''I have an idea,'' Eb suggested. ''About how we could kill just these cows, I mean.''

''How?''

Eb pointed to a steep cliff which formed one side of a

nearby gully. About halfway up the cliff a large rock jutted out from the side. It seemed to be positioned to hold back the top half of the wall.

"What do you think would happen if we put some blastin' powder right there under that rock?" he asked.

"It would bring down that entire side," Win said.

"And with the cows trapped in the draw below, it would kill them and bury them at the same time," Joe said, picking up on it as well. "Eb's right, Win, it would work."

"All right, let's do it," Win said.

"God, I'm goin' to hate killin' all them cows like that," Eb said. "It's almost like murder."

"We're going to have to kill them anyway, Eb, you said so yourself," Win said. "Don't look at it as to how many cows we might kill. Look at it as to how many we can save."

"I know you're right," Eb admitted. "I just hate it that we have to do it, that's all."

"And I hate the sons of bitches that's caused this," Joe growled.

"Listen, we're going to have to keep them inside until we can set the powder," Win said. "Joe, you think you and Eb could drive them in there, then build a little barricade that will keep them from wandering back out?"

"Yeah, we can do that," Joe said, answering for himself and Eb.

"All right, you two do that, and I'll ride back to the ranch and see if I can find some powder."

"They's some kegs of blasting powder in a shed out behind the barn," Eb said.

"What if Cherokee sees you taking the powder?" Joe asked. "What will you tell him?"

"I'll tell him we're blasting out a well," Win suggested.

The ride to the ranch and back took an hour, and by the time Win returned he saw that Joe and Eb had done their job well. The cattle had been herded into the gully, and a barricade of rocks, limbs, and sagebrush kept them securely pinned inside.

"Joe!" Win called. "Where are you?"

"They are up here with me, Mr. Coulter," a strange voice answered, and Win, startled by the outside voice, reined up sharply. Ahead he saw four men riding down the side of the hill toward him. Three of the men were wearing badges and carrying rifles. The fourth was wearing a suit. Behind the four men, he saw Joe and Eb, and the expressions on their faces showed anger and frustration.

"Who the hell are you?" Win asked the man wearing the suit.

"My name is Parker, Dr. Rufus Parker. I am a veterinarian."

"A veterinarian? We didn't send for a veterinarian."

"I daresay you didn't," Parker said. "And from the looks of things, you would have, no doubt, preferred that I not come."

"What are you doing out here?" Win asked.

"I am doing my duty, sir. I was told by an anonymous source that there may be a danger of hoof-and-mouth exposure on Camelot so I rode out here to see for myself."

"You must have left in the middle of the night to get here," Win said. "Do you put that much store in something an anonymous source told you?"

"I assure you, sir, I have as much disdain for an anonymous source as do you. But such an allegation is too serious to overlook. And, in this case, I see that the allegation was correct," Parker replied. "I have found one cow who is in the advanced stages of the disease."

"And did you, by chance, notice that the cow was wearing a different brand?" Win asked.

"Yes, your brother pointed that out to me. He also suggested that the cow might have been purposely put into the herd."

"No *might* have been to it, Dr. Parker. It *was* put into the herd," Win said. "Someone has deliberately set about to infect Mr. Wellington's cows."

"I'm sorry, but that doesn't change anything. The animals still must be destroyed."

"I know," Win said with a sigh. He pointed to the two kegs of blasting powder he had brought with him. "That's why we were going to destroy these animals.''

"Not just these animals," Parker said. "According to the law, you are going to have to destroy every animal on the ranch.''

"That law don't make no sense," Win said. He pointed toward the east. "This is a big ranch, and the cows are scattered in small bunches all over the place. Hell, some of Emmerline's cows are closer to this herd than the rest of Wellington's animals.''

Parker looked at Win for a moment, then he stroked his chin, as if he were deep in thought.

"Yes," he finally said. "Yes, you do have a point there. All right, I am taking a terrible risk, but, for now, destroy these cows only.''

"Thanks," Win answered with a sigh of relief.

"But we are going to keep a very close watch on all the rest of the animals," Parker went on. "In no way shall any of them be allowed to come into contact with animals from beyond the boundaries of this ranch.''

"That could be a problem," Joe said.

"In what way?" Dr. Parker asked. "All you have to do is keep Wellington's cows on the ranch and not let any other cows come into contact with them.''

"That's where the problem is," Win said. "As you may know, Emmerline has dammed up Gypsum River, cutting all the other ranchers off from a source of water. Mr. Wellington is letting his neighbors bring their cows onto Camelot.''

"And they've been doing that all along?" Parker asked.

"Yes," Win said. "Of course, some of them are goin' onto the Double-Diamond and paying Emmerline a third of their cows to use his water.''

"Wait a minute," Parker said, holding up his hand. "Are you telling me that some ranchers bring their cows over here to water, then those same cows might go onto the Double-Diamond?''

"They not only go over there, a third of them stay there," Win said.

"My God," Parker said. "With that kind of intermixing

of the herds, the entire range has been exposed! I had no idea of the magnitude of this. If we do things to the letter of the law, we will have to slaughter tens of thousands. That would be a catastrophe of unimaginable proportions.''

''Then we're going to have to find some other way of handling it,'' Win suggested. He pointed to the kegs of powder. ''What if we just close off this gully like we were planning?''

''No, no,'' Parker said, shaking his head. ''We can't get away with that.''

''So what are you plannin' on doin', Doc? Killin' ever' cow in the panhandle?'' Eb asked.

''No,'' Parker replied. He pinched the bridge of his nose. ''No, I don't want to do that either.'' Mumbling to himself, he started back toward his horse. Just before he mounted, he turned around to look at Win and the others. ''I'll see what I can work out. In the meantime, we can't take a chance on any of these cows getting out, so go ahead and take care of them just as you planned.''

''Parker?'' Win called as Parker mounted and started to ride away. Parker stopped and looked back toward him.

''You're a good man,'' Win said.

''My intentions are good,'' Parker replied. ''Let's just hope that the results aren't disastrous.''

15

DR. RUFUS PARKER WAS A GRADUATE OF THE SCHOOL OF veterinary medicine at Cornell University. He had served in the Federal Army during the Civil War, and at the end of the war found himself in Texas. Unlike so many other ex-Yankees and carpetbaggers who stayed in the defeated South because they saw opportunity there, Dr. Rufus Parker stayed because he fell in love with Texas. He was entranced by the wide-open spaces, the rugged but beautiful country, and the men and women who were as tough as the country they inhabited. And, as a veterinarian, he felt that he could be of some benefit to his adopted home.

Now all of that, his love of the state, his sense of duty, and his eagerness to do well, was under fire.

At one point during his time in the army Parker was put in charge of procuring and certifying the health of every mount in the entire U.S. Cavalry. He was sure he would never again face a responsibility so great. But the responsibility he faced now at least equaled, and perhaps surpassed that. The law, regarding what he should do, was very clear. But the framers of the law could never have anticipated a situation where all the cattle of all the ranchers were so intermixed.

Arguing for some leniency, Dr. Parker carried the plight of the ranchers to the Texas Cattle Commission. There, after a long consultation and several detailed negotiations, the Cattle Commission agreed to grant Parker the flexibility he sought. Not every animal would have to be killed. However, and this was where the onus came down on Parker, every animal known to be or suspected to be directly exposed to the disease would have to be destroyed.

"You understand, do you not, Doctor, that the fate of an entire industry depends upon your good judgment?" the head of the Commission charged.

"I understand, sir," Parker replied. "And you may rest assured that I will do my duty."

Although the Texas Cattle Commission granted a waiver which saved many thousands of head of cattle, the number of animals that would have to be destroyed was still quite significant. When Parker issued the order it had a tremendous effect upon not only the ranchers, but everyone whose livelihood directly or indirectly depended upon the ranchers. And, in this part of Texas, that was everyone.

The destroy order as it pertained to Camelot included the small herd that Win, Joe, and Eb had already killed and buried in the gully, as well as three more nearby herds. The final count of Phillip Wellington's animals to be disposed of was a little over six hundred head. In addition, approximately one hundred cows from Tony Kindig's herd, and another one hundred from Clyde Carter's were included, plus an aggregate of just under a hundred from all the other ranchers who had, to a lesser degree, accepted Wellington's offer of water. The order also called for five hundred head of Double-Diamond cattle to be slaughtered.

Once the notifications went out, all the ranchers who were so notified were called to a meeting in the assembly room of the Cattlemen's Association, located behind the bank, in Loraine.

"By God, I don't mind tellin' you fellas, losing a hundred head of cattle is just about going to do me in," Tony Kindig complained to the others.

"Hell, Tony, by rights you should only have to give up sixty-six head," Clyde suggested.

"What do you mean?"

"Ain't Emmerline takin' a third of your action?" he asked.

The other ranchers laughed, and even Tony got a chuckle out of the black humor.

"Yeah, how about that, Emmerline? Suppose I give you sixty-six cows and you give up the rest?"

"I'm givin' up enough of my own cattle," Emmerline answered, not joining in the laughter. "Five hundred cows at forty dollars a head is twenty thousand dollars. And all because, out of the goodness of my heart, I granted you and some of my neighbors access to water."

"You ain't granting anybody anything," Clyde said. "What you are doing is charging them for water that you stole. And as far as I'm concerned you got what's comin' to you. The only thing I regret is that you aren't havin' to destroy your entire herd."

Emmerline glared at Clyde but said nothing.

"Wellington, is it true that the cow that brought the disease in was wearin' a strange brand, one that ain't from around here?" one of the smaller ranchers asked.

"Yes," Wellington replied. "It was carrying the Rocking S, a brand we have since learned is used by one Mr. Jeremy Sawyer, of Dallas."

"Dallas? How did an animal all the way from Dallas get in with your cows?"

"I believe it was purposely introduced," Wellington replied.

"Purposely introduced, you say? What makes you think that?" Emmerline asked.

"A couple of my hands were watching over the herd one night when they encountered what they thought were rustlers," Wellington said. "They shot at them and ran them off. Then later they realized that they weren't trying to rustle at all, but were, instead, putting the infected cow in with my herd."

"These hands you are talking about, they aren't working cowboys, are they?" Emmerline asked.

"They work for me," Wellington answered without being more specific.

"But they aren't cowboys?" Emmerline repeated.

"They are jacks-of-all-trades. They repair equipment, dig wells, and protect my daughter. They are what the railroad people call troubleshooters."

"It is true, is it not, that in 'protecting' your daughter, they killed four men?"

"Yes," Wellington agreed hesitantly. "But it is my understanding that they had no choice. And they did bring my daughter back safely to me."

"They are gunmen, aren't they?" Emmerline accused.

"Who are you to talk about hiring a gunman?" Clyde asked. "Ain't it true that you've hired this maggot Shardeen?"

"Yes, what about that?" one of the others asked. "What is Shardeen, if he ain't a gunman?"

"What makes you think Shardeen is a gunman?" Emmerline asked.

"He's killed two of my men," Clyde said.

"In self-defense," Emmerline replied.

"Bullshit!" Clyde thundered. "That pasty-faced son of a bitch goaded them into drawing on him. Hell, all the witnesses say as much."

"Those same eyewitnesses say that your men drew first."

"Now he hangs out in the Black Horse in town, near about ever' night, trying to fight with our hands," another man added.

"Gentlemen," Emmerline said in an oil-smooth voice. "If your men are picking fights in the saloons, it is, no doubt, because they are trying to prove something. I would advise them, however, not to attempt to pick a fight with Shardeen. Of course he is skilled with a firearm, that's why I hired him. But I didn't hire him as a gunman, nor even as a troubleshooter. I hired him as a bodyguard."

"Bodyguard?"

"Yes, bodyguard. Is that so unusual? It certainly should come as no surprise to you gentlemen to learn that I am a very wealthy man. That means that there are many who would attack me, and rob me, if they could. But as long as

Mr. Shardeen is in my employ, no one would dare.''

Shardeen, who had been the object of the spirited discussion, stood over by the wall with his arms folded across his chest. His gun was worn low and kicked out in the way of a gunman, and he was as totally disdainful of the ranchers' discussion of him as if they had been talking about the weather.

''On the other hand, Phillip, the two men that you have hired, these Coulter brothers, are quite dangerous indeed. Are you aware that they were members of Quantrill's Raiders? That is the most infamous band of cutthroats and brigands ever assembled.''

''I am aware that they fought with Quantrill,'' Wellington replied. ''But I am also aware that there are many in the South who don't consider Quantrill a brigand at all, but rather regard him as a true cavalier for the Confederate cause.''

Wellington's response was met with a barrage of cheers from the other ranchers, nearly all of whom had fought in the recent war on the side of the South. Emmerline waited until the cheers subsided before he continued his argument.

''Regardless of the perceived merits or faults of the two men in question, they were hired by you to look for trouble. Isn't that right?''

Wellington paused for a moment before he answered. ''Yes,'' he finally said.

''Then don't you think that it is entirely possible that the Coulter brothers might have, themselves, introduced a diseased animal to your herd?''

''No. Why in heaven's name would they do such a thing?''

''Perhaps they thought it would make them look more important in your eyes,'' Emmerline suggested.

''I have no reason to doubt them.''

''What is it you are gettin' at, Emmerline?'' Tony asked. ''Do you have some other idea as to where that animal might have come from?''

''As a matter of fact, I do,'' Emmerline replied.

"Then, by all means, share it with us," Wellington challenged.

"I was waiting for you to ask," Emmerline said. He smiled smugly and held up a piece of paper. "Gentlemen, this is a bill of lading. According to this document, Mr. Wellington took receipt, by rail shipment, of twenty head of cattle, four weeks ago. The point of origin for the cattle was Dallas, Texas. And, as we have just been told, the diseased cow came from Dallas, Texas."

There were several exclamations of surprise from the other ranchers, and a few shouted curses and accusations. Dr. Parker, who had been conducting the meeting, had to bang the gavel repeatedly to restore order.

"That is a very reckless accusation, Mr. Emmerline," Wellington said in an angry, clipped voice.

"What about it, Wellington?" one of the other ranchers called out. "Did you have them cows shipped in or not?"

"Gentlemen, the twenty head of cattle on that bill of lading are all blooded brood bulls. I assure you, the pathetic creature we found on the range would not come under that category."

"Yes, well, how are we going to prove that now?" Emmerline asked. "The animal in question has already been conveniently destroyed and disposed of. And no one saw it but your men."

"That's not true," Wellington replied. "Dr. Parker also saw it."

"Is that true, Dr. Parker?" Tony asked. "Did you see the infected cow?"

"Yes, I saw the animal."

"Do you think it was one of the blooded brood bulls Wellington is talking about?"

"It was a bull," Parker agreed. "But its condition was so deteriorated that it is difficult to judge as to whether it would have been one of the blooded bulls Mr. Wellington is talking about."

"Oh, come now. You're a veterinarian, ain't you? Are you tellin' me you couldn't tell whether it was a blooded bull or not?" one of the ranchers demanded.

"I'm sorry," Parker said. "As I said, its condition was too far gone for me to be able to judge."

"Hell, I don't need you to judge," Tony said. "If Phillip Wellington says the diseased animal wasn't one of the cows he shipped in, then that's good enough for me."

"Mr. Kindig, for your faith and confidence in me, you have my most sincere appreciation," Wellington said.

"Dr. Parker, may I make a motion?" one of the other ranchers asked.

"Yes, please do," Parker answered. The meeting was becoming difficult.

"If that cow really is from Dallas, it sure as hell didn't walk here. And if it didn't come in with the twenty that Wellington says he bought, then it must've come in by itself. Why don't you check with the railroad and see where it come from, and who it went to."

"I shall do so," Parker promised.

"Which brings us right back to where we was," Clyde said.

"And that is?" Parker asked.

"That somebody put that cow onto Camelot for the pure purpose of infecting all of Camelot's cattle."

"Yeah, only when they did it, they got our cows too," one of the other ranchers added.

"So all we need to do now is find out who the bastard is, then string him up!" someone shouted.

"Yeah!" the others responded in a loud yell.

"If you ask me," Clyde said, "we don't have to look no further than to find out who stands to gain and who stands to lose in this deal."

"Gain? Who could possibly gain from such a thing?" Tony asked.

Clyde looked directly at Emmerline. "Maybe somebody who figures that he can pick up our ranches real cheap if we all lose our herds."

"See here!" Emmerline sputtered, pointing at Clyde. "Are you accusing me? You have no right to say such a thing!"

"I reckon I've got a right to call a skunk a skunk when

I see one," Clyde said. "And if you don't care for my remarks, Emmerline, you can always call me out."

"Here, here, hold on now!" Dr. Parker shouted, holding his hands up in an effort to quiet the situation. "There's no need for all that! There will be nobody calling anybody out. Now, gentlemen, we have a bad situation facing us here and the only way we are going to get through it is by cooperating with one another. The bad news is, you are going to have to kill some cattle. But the good news is, you don't have to destroy your entire herds."

"Here, here," Wellington said. He stood up and looked at the other assembled ranchers. "Gentlemen, regardless of how this diseased animal got onto my ranch, it did get there, and thus exposed not only my cattle but some of yours as well. For that, I deeply apologize. But," he pointed toward Dr. Parker, "let us not, in our frustration, lose sight of what Dr. Parker has done for us. He has saved thousands of animals from a senseless and wasteful slaughter, and I think we owe him our appreciation, and a round of applause."

The ranchers applauded and, in their common cause, some of the bitterness passed.

"Gentlemen, you all know the arrangement," Parker said. "For the most part you will be on your honor. I ask you not to violate that trust, but to bring every cow that you know or even suspect may have been exposed to the field designated on the maps you received when you arrived today. And I thank you in advance for your cooperation."

IN ORDER TO BRING ABOUT A MORE EFFICIENT OPERATION, all the affected cattle from all the ranches were gathered in one large, open field on public land. On the day appointed, cowboys from all the ranches drove their herds to the designated place. The operation had all the trappings of a regular spring roundup, and, despite the solemnity of the occasion, there was a sense of excitement to the event. As Win and Joe approached they could hear the sounds of the drive, the bawling and crying of cattle, and the shouts and whistles of the wranglers before they could actually make anything out in the dust cloud.

Finally they could see the cows moving forward relentlessly, prodded on by the drovers. The two brothers rode around the edge of the growing herd, keeping out of everyone's way as they headed for the chuck wagon. The chuck wagon, they knew, would be the headquarters of the drive, and there they saw Dr. Parker and several of his assistants making a careful inventory, by owner, of all the cows that were brought in.

The count served two purposes. It would assess the amount of damage done by the outbreak, and it would also determine the compensation to be paid to the cattlemen for the animals they were forced to destroy. Though the compensation was minuscule compared to the losses they were actually sustaining, it was a source of badly needed revenue for some of the smaller ranchers.

By early afternoon more than a hundred men, dressed in long white coats and wearing bandannas, were ready to go about the grim work of slaughter. This impromptu army was composed of cowboys from all the ranches except those that were affected.

"You boys about ready?" Dr. Parker called to them.

The lead cowboy, a foreman from a ranch in the next county, nodded, then jacked a round into the chamber of his rifle and started toward the herd.

"Let's go, boys," he called to the others.

There was the sound of a score or more rifles being cocked, then, a moment later, the first bang.

Immediately after the first shot came a dozen more, then more yet, so that it quickly took on the sound of a battlefield, with rifles roaring, men shouting, cattle bawling then falling over.

Gun smoke drifted over the tightly gathered herd, and the smell of expended powder joined the odor of cow manure and the sickeningly sweet smell of fear.

The cowboys who had brought the cattle in, the same ones who had rounded them up as calves, branded them, and worked them for the past few years, now stood by and watched the killing. Their faces were pinched, their eyes squinted, and they smoked, or stood by in silence, deploring what was going on but unable to take their eyes off the massacre.

The killing went on with grim efficiency. The animals would be shot, then dragged into one of several large pits which had been dug nearby. The pits were lined with lime, and as the cows were tossed into the pits they too would be covered with lime.

Like the other hands from Camelot, Win and Joe were taking no part in the actual slaughter, but were standing near the chuck wagon, watching silently. Dr. Parker came over to draw himself a cup of coffee, then he turned to watch as the shooting continued.

"Gruesome business, this," Parker said.

"Yeah," Joe grunted.

"All the more gruesome when you realize that it was a deliberate attempt to infect the herd," Parker said. He pulled a letter from his jacket pocket. "I got this letter from Mr. Sawyer this morning, confirming that he was, indeed, the source of the diseased cow."

Joe looked at him in surprise. "What? You mean the son of a bitch admitted it?"

"He admits shipping the cow out here by rail."

"Who did he send it to?" Win asked.

"Yes, well, now that is the mystery," Parker answered. "Mr. Sawyer claims he was contacted by a representative of West Texas Normal and offered top dollar for a hoof-and-mouth infected animal to be used in their college of veterinary medicine for research."

"Where is West Texas Normal?"

"That's just it," Parker replied. "There is no such school."

"All right, who picked up the cow at the depot?"

Parker shook his head. "I wasn't able to get an answer to that question," he said. "I checked. The freight master remembers seeing the bill of lading, but, according to his records, the cow was never claimed. Whoever got it must've sneaked down to the train yard in the middle of the night and taken it off the car. I'd sure like to find out who it was."

"Yeah," Win said menacingly. "I'd like to find out too."

"Dr. Parker," someone called, "you want to come over here a minute?"

"Would you gentlemen excuse me, please?" Parker asked as he left to respond to the call. As Parker was leaving, Eb Peters came over to pour himself a cup of coffee. Eb was one of the cowboys who had brought in the Camelot herd.

"Listen to them sons of bitches," Eb growled, taking in the shooters with a wave of his arm. "By God, I think some of those bastards are actually enjoying this. Listen to 'em yell."

Eb was referring to the frequent "yahoos!" and occasional Rebel yells that could be heard through the incessant banging of the rifles.

"They think it's like hunting buffalo or something," Eb said.

"It could've been worse," Win said.

"Yeah, I guess so. My God, can you imagine if we'd had to kill ever' cow on the place? And the other ranches besides?" Eb replied. He took a swallow of coffee and looked out toward the herd.

Suddenly a steer broke loose from the herd and dashed through the line of shooters, heading at a dead run toward the chuck wagon.

"Stop him! Get him!" someone shouted.

Eb leaped into the saddle of his horse and started after the steer. Bringing his horse right alongside the terrified critter, he leaned over from his saddle, then, grabbing the animal by the horns, leaped from his horse. Digging his boots into the ground he let the steer drag him for a few feet, then the animal came to a stop and Eb twisted its neck around, bringing it down.

Shortly after that Gus arrived with a rope. He threw the rope to Eb, and Eb dropped it around the steer's head so it could be led back into the herd.

"Wait a minute!" Eb called, just before Gus started back toward the herd with it.

"What is it?" Gus asked.

"Look at this ear," Eb said, pointing to the animal's ear. "Ain't this . . ." Eb stopped and looked at the brand. "No, it can't be," he said. "Still, it . . ."

"Gus! Get that cow back with the others!" Cherokee suddenly shouted.

"Cherokee, this here cow looks like . . ." Eb started, but by now Cherokee had ridden over, and he took the lariat from Gus, then put his horse into a gallop, forcing the steer to run back into the herd.

"Shoot this son of a bitch before it runs away again!" Cherokee shouted, and the closest shooter brought the steer down with one shot.

Cherokee rode back to Eb, who was still standing there, looking on in surprise at the foreman's odd behavior.

"I don't know what you saw, or think you saw," Cherokee growled. He pointed back toward the herd. "But whatever it was, forget about it. We're out here to see to it that them cows get killed. Now, if you ain't quite got the stomach for it, you go on back to the ranch."

"I was just—" Eb started.

"I don't care what you was just," Cherokee interrupted. "These men have a hard enough job to do without you gettin' in their way."

Cherokee slapped his legs against the sides of his horse and galloped away, headed for a distant part of the herd.

Duly chastised, Eb remounted, then rode back over to the chuck wagon, from which Win and Joe had witnessed the entire scene.

"Good job of bulldogging the steer," Joe offered, as Eb dismounted.

"Thanks," Eb replied. He looked sullenly toward Cherokee, who was now small in the distance. "I sure as hell don't know what he was all riled up over."

"What were you talking about?" Win asked.

"That's just it," Eb said. "I didn't get a chance to talk

at all. But if I had, I would've pointed out somethin' that's a mite peculiar.''

"What's that?''

"That steer I just run down had a strange right ear. Actually, you might say it had three strange right ears.''

"Three ears? What are you talking about?''

"The right ear,'' Eb said. "It ain't one ear at all. It's three separate, very small, but perfectly formed ears. I remember seeing it when I branded it as a calf a couple of years ago.'' He laughed. "I recall that me 'n Pete was goin' to see if we could buy 'im off Mr. Wellington. We was goin' to take 'im back east and show 'im off at county fairs an' the like, then get rich.''

"And that's one of 'em we're havin' to kill,'' Joe said. "I'm sorry.''

"No, that ain't it,'' Eb said. "Well, that too, but the funny thing about that cow was the brand it was wearin'.''

"What about the brand?''

"It was a Double-Diamond brand,'' Eb said. "I know damn well that was the same cow. What I don't know is why it was wearin' the Double-Diamond brand.''

"Hey, Eb! You wanna give us a hand over here?'' someone called, and Eb excused himself and went over to offer his assistance to the cowboy who'd called him.

Win waited until Eb and the others were gone, then he squatted down and picked up a stick and started scratching in the dirt.

"What are you doin'?'' Joe asked.

"Look at this,'' Win replied.

Win scratched a *W* in the dirt. "What is that?'' he asked.

"It's a W. Camelot's brand,'' Joe said.

"Yes. Now, look at this.'' Win stood up, then walked around to the other side of the *W* he had scratched in the ground. He made another *W*, but from the opposite direction. The second *W* he put right on top of the first.

"What do you think it is now?'' he asked.

"I'll be damned,'' Joe answered, looking at the brand his brother had just completed drawing. "It's the Double-Diamond.''

16

JULIE DIPPED A CLOTH IN THE BUCKET OF WATER, THEN began washing the blackboards in the single-room schoolhouse. The woman who had taught school the year before had gotten married during the summer, and the Loraine school board offered the job to Julie. Julie took it, not so much from the need of an income, as a need to keep herself gainfully occupied.

The job also provided a small living quarters at the back of the school, and although Julie had enjoyed her stay with Pamela, she was looking forward to a place of her own.

There was another advantage to having her own place. She could entertain Joe Coulter. Of course, she would have to be very, very discreet, because as the schoolmarm, she couldn't afford the slightest hint of a scandal. There would be a risk, to be sure, but it was worth it. She recalled the night she'd visited Joe in his little room behind the toolshed out on Camelot, and her blood warmed and her breathing grew shallow. Oh, how wonderful it had been . . . and how much she wished she could do it again. If only he were here, right now, they could pull the shades and lock the doors. No one would see them, no one would know.

As she suddenly realized the extent and the intensity of her thoughts, her face flamed in embarrassment. Trying to push the thoughts aside lest they drive her into distraction, she dipped the cloth in the bucket and began washing the blackboard with renewed vigor. She covered the board with broad sweeps, watching the slate grow black under each pass as the white film of chalk was cleaned away.

ACROSS THE STREET FROM THE SCHOOL, LUCAS SHARDEEN stood just inside the livery stable. The bottom half of the door was closed and he leaned on it, looking through the open top half. From here, he had discovered, he could see into the school, and he could watch Julie Vincent, without her knowing she was being watched.

In the week since Julie Vincent had moved to town and begun preparation for the start of school, she had spoken to Shardeen only in the most perfunctory way. Sometimes he would watch carefully, judging exactly when she would leave the school, then he would hurry to get into position to walk by her. He always made it a point to tip his hat and speak, and she answered him with a polite nod of her head, but never once had they exchanged any pleasantries.

Who does she think she is? he wondered. Men quaked in their boots when he spoke to them. He once made a six-foot-tall, powerfully built man get on his knees and beg for his life. Even now, as he recalled that moment, he relished the thought of reducing such a fine specimen of manhood to a quivering lump of jelly.

Then he blew his brains out.

"You are in that schoolhouse all alone some evenin's, ain't you, missy?" Shardeen said under his breath. "Well, little miss high-and-mighty bitch, let's see what you're like some late night when you think you're safe, when there's nobody around for you to turn to. I'll just pay you a visit, and you'll notice me then. Yes, ma'am, I can guarantee that you will notice me.

"The first thing I'm going to do is make sure that you know I'm the one who killed your uncle. Then after you learn that little bit of information, I'll tell you what I have planned for you."

As he did when he saw her the first time, Shardeen reached down to grab himself. Now, however, in the privacy of an end stall in the stable, he didn't have to feel himself through his trousers. Now he was able to unbutton his fly and pull out the snow-white piece of flesh.

"You'll beg me not to kill you. You'll offer to let me use you any way I want. But all your beggin' and all your offers won't do you any good."

Shardeen began to masturbate. "No, ma'am," he said as he whipped the skin back and forth in a frenzy. "It won't do you any good a'tall."

BACK AT CAMELOT, PAMELA STOOD IN HER ROOM AT THE mirror and studied her reflection. How different her world was here from what it had been in England! There she had been a schoolgirl with only the most remote notion of life. Now she was experiencing life to its fullest.

And yet one thing persisted.

As an English schoolgirl her life was orderly and ordered. She knew exactly who she was and what her station in life was. She never thought about men except in some vague, romantic way, taken from novels of knights in shining armor rescuing fair young damsels.

She never thought that *she* would be rescued by some knight in shining armor, because her own future was already planned. She was engaged to Sir Edward Ticely, son of the Duke of Wimberly. Sir Edward was actually her second cousin, and the marriage had been arranged by her father and the Duke of Wimberly when she was only twelve years old. She had only seen him once in the last ten years.

Although Sir Edward was her fiancé, and as far as she knew, the arrangement was still in effect, Pamela never thought of him in any sort of erotic way. Not in the way she thought of Win Coulter.

As Pamela thought of Win now her skin flushed and she felt a fluttering inside. She had never experienced anything like the sensations she felt when Win made love to her. Oh, how wonderful it would be, she thought, if she could marry Win Coulter instead of Sir Edward Ticely.

Of course, that could never be. Win Coulter was a common cowboy . . . no, not even a cowboy. He and his brother

were drifters, with no more attachment to the land than the
tumbleweed the late, hot August winds rolled across the
prairie. Pamela was a titled Lady, and even though there
were no such things as titles in America, there was, nevertheless, a rigid recognition of the class system. Americans
gave lip service to all men being created equal, but money,
position, social standing, race, and religion separated Americans into classes as rigidly as did the peerage system in
England.

No matter how one looked at it, Win Coulter, a gunman
who once rode for Quantrill, a man nearly everyone called
a bandit, was not in Pamela's social class. And, even if
Pamela would step out of her class for him, she knew,
intuitively, that he would never leave his class for her.

Pamela leaned forward to study her face more closely in
the mirror. Then, looking deep into her own eyes, she spoke
aloud.

"Well, bloody hell, I don't want to marry him. I just
want to sleep with him."

She laughed at her own bawdy candidness.

HALF AN HOUR LATER PAMELA, ALREADY MOUNTED, AP-
peared at the corral. Win was saddling his horse.

"Well, I must say I am hurt," Pamela said.

Win looked around in confusion.

"Beg your pardon?"

"I said I am hurt," Pamela said. "Here, I asked you to
take me on a ride around the ranch to show me the location
of all the wells, and when I get here, you aren't even ready
to go."

Win pulled out the gold pocket watch that had been his
father's and looked at it.

"You said four o'clock," he said. "It's five minutes until."

"Oh? Well, then, perhaps I am the anxious one," Pamela
said with a little laugh.

Win tightened the cinch, then swung into the saddle and
smiled over at her. "All right," he said. "Let's go."

An hour later, when they were some distance away, a

great billowing rain cloud built up in the west.

"Damn!" Win said. "Isn't this the way of it, though? Here we've been breaking our backs gettin' in these wells and now it rains."

"Yes, but after the rain is gone and the puddles dry up, the cattle will still be here, and they will still need water," Pamela said.

"You're right about that," Win agreed. "In the meantime, we'd better go look for some shelter somewhere. Sometimes these summer storms can be real humdingers."

Win helped Pamela get her poncho on, then he put his own on and spread them both out to provide as much protection for the horses as he could.

"Let's go," he called out, and he led the way, moving off in a fast trot.

The dark, ominous clouds moved closer to them, preceded by swiftly moving tumbleweed and a rolling column of dust. Win and Pamela leaned forward in their saddles and hurried on.

Moments later the rains came, hitting them full force. At first, Win thought they would try to make it all the way back to the house, but the rain was coming with such velocity that the drops were actually stinging. Then a few minutes after the rain started it began to hail, and the horses grew frightened. That was when Win saw the line shack.

"Over there!" he called against the force of the storm.

Alongside the shack was a small lean-to for the horses, and Win tied them there. Then Win took Pamela by the hand and they darted through the storm to the weather-beaten shack.

"It appears cozy enough," Pamela said once they were inside. "It isn't even leaking."

Win looked around at the little line shack. It had a real tick mattress on the bed, a table and two chairs, and a combination cooking and heating stove. There was also a cabinet with several tins of fruits and vegetables, some dry beans, and coffee.

"They keep it well stocked, don't they?" Pamela said.

"Yes, well, I suppose when they have to stay out here they like it to be comfortable," Win said.

"Would you like me to make some coffee?"

"I thought you didn't like coffee."

"I don't."

"I hate to drink alone."

"You won't be alone. I'll be here with you," Pamela said, smiling at him.

"All right then, fine, I'd love some."

"I'll get right on it."

With Pamela puttering around in the kitchen, Win stepped out onto the front porch to watch the rain move across the mesa and slash into the prairie. A prairie dog, driven from one hole by quickly rising water, bounded along through the rain and disappeared down into another.

Though Win was sheltered from the direct effect of the rain, he was being splashed with the spray, but he made no attempt to escape. He liked the rain. It blanketed all sight and sound, and formed a curtain behind which his soul could exist in absolute solitude. Only those with whom he really wanted to share could penetrate it.

The front door opened and Pamela came out onto the porch to join him. She was carrying two steaming cups and handed one to him.

"You're going to drink coffee?" Win asked.

"Try it."

Win tasted it, then frowned. "This isn't coffee."

"No," Pamela said, smiling brightly. "Isn't it wonderful! I found some tea!"

Win took another swallow. "It's all right," he said. "Though, right now, I'd probably drink hot water and be satisfied."

Pamela looked out over the rain-swept prairie. "Oh, I know it is inconvenient," she said. "But I just love the rain. It reminds me of England. It rains often in England."

"Well, it may rain more in England, but I'll bet we have bigger storms," Win said.

"Yes, you do. You have wonderful, glorious storms," Pamela said, and she hugged herself as she leaned out to let some of the rain splash in her face. She laughed, then drew back out of the rain and looked at him, her face now spattered with droplets of water. Their eyes held for a moment, then she put her hand on his face, running her fingers along his jawline.

"Do you know that, in my country, we would never have even had the opportunity to meet?"

"I reckon not, seein' as I've never been to England," Win answered.

Pamela laughed. "No, I don't mean that. I mean if we both lived in England and we were both . . . as we are now."

Win smiled crookedly. "You mean, you bein' a princess and me bein' a peasant?"

"Well, I'm not a princess and you aren't a peasant," Pamela replied with a little laugh. "But, yes, something like that." She ran her hand around his jawline, down his neck, and then down inside his shirt, against his bare skin. "And that would have been a shame," she said. "For we would have never been able to swive."

"Swive?"

Pamela smiled at him seductively. "I think you probably know it by another, rather pithy word," she said. "One that starts with an 'F.' "

"Oh."

Pamela leaned into him and they kissed. Her tongue darted into his mouth as his hands moved to the front of her dress to begin working on the buttons. She leaned away from him then and with the same seductive smile on her face looked up at him.

"If we are going to have a bit of a swive, and I certainly hope that we are, then I would prefer to do it inside," she said.

Laughing, Win held open the door.

"After you, m'lady," he said.

Pamela giggled. "Oh, you do play the game well."

Once inside, it took but a few moments for them to get undressed and onto the tick mattress on the bed. Then Win lay beside her and pulled her naked body close against his own. Despite the slight chill in the air, her flesh was warm with desire.

"My mind tells me not to throw myself at you so," Pamela said. "For I know you must think me the slattern. But, God help me, I can't help myself."

Win said nothing, but he allowed his lips and hands to seek out the areas that would bring her pleasure. Pamela's sighs of ecstasy turned to eager moans, and her body began to writhe beside him. She thrust her breasts up urgently to receive the attentions of his active tongue, and his fingers slipped into a silky moistness as they pushed even deeper within her. Each time his finger slid across her quivering clitoris, the muscles of her lower abdomen contracted in an involuntary expression of enjoyment.

After a few moments of such foreplay, Win, now fully erect and ready, moved over her, then eased himself down inside. Pamela's back arched, and her tongue slipped out to lick her own lips as she received him. An all-consuming feeling of pleasure surged up from Win's loins as he sunk into her hot, damp depths.

"Ohhh, that's wonderful," Pamela said, the words little more than a shuddering moan.

Win pulled out of her slightly, then pushed in again, drifting with the waves of pleasure that were renewed with each stroke.

For a few moments Pamela lay still, letting Win establish the rhythm of their copulation. But she couldn't lay still for long. Eventually her lower body began to arch of its own accord, and she rose to meet his every thrust. She reached her first climax with an ease that amazed Win, then she lay still for a couple of minutes as he plunged on.

But she came again, when he did.

They lay together for a few moments, listening to the rain outside, then Pamela raised herself on one elbow and looked down at him. The motion flattened one of her breasts and made a pear-shaped pendulum of the other.

"Would you think it terribly crass of me if I suggested that we do it again?" she asked.

"Again? Well, give me some time to get ready and I'll do what I can to accommodate you."

"Oh, I'll give you more than time," Pamela said. "I'll give you some help." And, to Win's pleasant surprise, she moved down to take him into her mouth.

Win put his hands into her hair as she worked on him, her lips moving up and down the length of his suddenly reawakened shaft, her tongue darting back and forth at the tip. After a minute or two of her ministrations Win spoke to her in a strained voice.

"Darlin', if you want to do again what we did a while ago, you'd best get up here and let me get to work."

"Work?" she asked, pulling her mouth away from him. "Is that what you call it?"

"Swive, work, whatever we call it, let's just do it," Win said.

They were so comfortable with each other now that there was no awkwardness of any kind. Pamela was eager to receive him, and she moved herself under him so he could fill her wet, waiting cavity.

Win began pumping into her with long, delectable thrusts that soon brought her to the brink of another orgasm. But this time, instead of carrying her on through, he stopped, leaving her hanging on the edge.

"No! What are you doing? Don't stop!" she pleaded, her voice husky with urgency.

"Wait," Win said.

Pamela lay beneath him, her insides twitching and aching for fulfillment. Win waited, unmoving, for her urgent moment to subside. Then, when all the twitching ceased, he started again. A moment later, when he sensed that she was ready again, he paused one more time.

"Win!" Pamela gasped. "What are you doing? Do you have any idea what you are doing to me?"

"Yeah," Win replied. "Some."

Again, Win waited for her twitchings to still, then, when once more her body had quieted, Win pulled himself almost all the way out of her. He held himself that way for just a moment, then he slammed his body forward, plunging deep into her, deeper than he had yet gone.

Pamela gasped with the unexpected pleasure of it, and her body began to throb and jump, partly from the impact of his thrusts into her, and partly from the thunderbolts of pleasure that flashed inside of her. This time, as she raced toward her orgasm, Win didn't hold back. He felt his own climax coming and he pushed himself up to the edge, felt it starting in the middle of his back, the soles of his feet, and the furnace of his loins. He began spewing hot jism inside her, and Pamela joined him, moaning and twitching in a mind-wracking orgasm.

When Pamela shuddered through the last convulsive moment of her orgasm, Win stayed over her, holding his weight off her but keeping them connected.

"Oh, that was so good," she finally breathed.

Win pulled himself out of her with a little smacking sound, then he lay alongside her. He said nothing for a long moment until he noticed that the rain which had driven them inside seeking shelter was over.

"The rain has stopped," he finally said.

"Win?"

Win raised himself up to look down at Pamela. To his surprise, he saw that she was crying.

"What is it?" he asked. "What's wrong?"

"Win, you know that nothing can ever come of this, don't you? I mean, all that talk about class differences. It's more than just talk. God help me, it's more than just talk."

"I know," Win said.

Pamela lifted her hand and again ran her fingers along his jawline.

"You don't hate me?"

"How can I hate anyone who has just given me so much pleasure?" Win replied.

Smiling now, Pamela sat up and wiped the tears from her eyes. "Yes, that's it, isn't it?" she finally said. "We have been able to give each other pleasure. And regardless of whatever happens, years from now, when I am married, and perhaps the matriarch of a large family . . . be they

American or British, I can always recall the pleasure of this moment.''

Pamela kissed Win on the cheek, then made a little face. ''I've been meaning to tell you,'' she said. ''You really should get a shave.''

17

THE RAIN, WHICH HAD BEEN FALLING INTERMITTENTLY throughout the day, began again that night. In her room at the rear of the schoolhouse Julie had already gone to bed. She lay there listening to the rain, watching the flashes of lightning through the window, shrinking before the crashing reports of thunder. Then, in between the thunder and the roar of rain, she heard a banging sound from the front of the schoolhouse. She lay still for a full moment longer, trying to ignore it, but she knew she couldn't. If the door had blown open she was going to have to close it right away. School would be starting in a few days, and she couldn't afford to have her books ruined by the rain.

With a sigh, Julie got up to investigate the source of the sound.

At first she thought she would take a candle. Then she decided she didn't want to waste the match. Besides, she had been working here now for the past two weeks, and she knew the classroom well enough to navigate it with her eyes closed.

The thunder boomed and the rain roared as Julie walked from her room, passing through the children's cloakroom, and out into the classroom. She stayed against the wall so as not to bump into any of the students' desks, and started picking her way toward the front door.

Halfway there, she stopped.

She hadn't heard or seen anything, but for some strange reason she began to experience the uneasy sensation that she wasn't alone. Her hair stood on end, and a hollowness began spreading from the pit of her stomach.

"Hello?" she called out tentatively. She waited for a moment but got no answer. "Hello, who's here?" she called again.

Still no answer.

The feeling grew stronger, and the uneasiness turned to outright fear.

"I know someone is here," she said, her voice nearly breaking. "Who is it? What do you want? If you are just looking to get out of the rain, please tell me. You are frightening me."

Suddenly there was a brilliant flash of lightning, a large bolt that illuminated everything for fully two seconds. The entire classroom was brightly lit, a world without color. She could see every object in the room with amazing clarity. She saw each desk standing out in bold relief, and the alphabet she had so carefully copied on the blackboard.

And she could see Shardeen, standing just inside the door. His albino complexion seemed even whiter in the flash of lightning, and he took on the appearance of an apparition from the bowels of hell itself.

The room went instantly black. Julie screamed, but her scream was drowned out by the crash of thunder that came immediately after the light died.

"Come here, bitch!" Shardeen shouted. He started to run toward her, but in the dark he hit his shin and tripped over one of the desks. He fell, cursing, to the floor.

Julie turned to run but stopped short of going into her room. She couldn't go in there because there was no door leading out and she would be trapped. The only way out of the building was by the front door, but she couldn't go that way without passing Shardeen. Julie got down on her hands and knees and started crawling, quickly, along the floor. She was just below the blackboard, and it was her intention to hide behind her desk.

No, she couldn't go there. That would be the first place he'd look!

She had to think!

She couldn't just go pell-mell around the room, she had to have some destination, some purpose! She had the presence of mind then to remember that there was a loose board right in front of her, so she moved around it, then crawled through the darkness to the opposite wall.

"Where are you, whore?" Shardeen called, his sibilant voice sounding like the hiss of a serpent. "I've got something for you." He giggled insanely. Another flash of lightning, neither as brilliant nor as long as the previous flash, lit the room dimly. From her position on the floor near the bookshelves, Julie could see that Shardeen was now holding a gun.

The light frightened her and she moved sharply, bumping into the shelf and knocking several books onto the floor. Shardeen heard her and looked over just as the light was dying. He got a fleeting glimpse of her and he fired, the flash from his pistol extending the illumination of the room for a split second.

The bullet crashed into a shelf near her, and splinters of wood flew from the impact. One little sliver hit her in the arm and she felt its sting.

"Make it easy for me and I'll make you like it," Shardeen called. He began moving across the room toward her, stumbling into one desk after another, cursing with each new obstacle.

Julie crawled quickly along the wall, heading toward the door.

"I made it easy for your uncle," Shardeen said. "I killed him quick."

"You . . . you killed him?" Julie gasped. She bit her tongue, for she realized, instantly, that she should have made no sound. But it was impossible not to react to Shardeen's almost casual comment about killing her father.

Shardeen smiled broadly. He had gotten just the response he wanted, and hearing her voice located her for him.

"Yeah, I killed him," he continued, baiting her. "But,

like I said, I made it easy for him. He didn't suffer none. He died just real quick. If you're nice to me, I'll make it easy for you, too . . . after,'' he added, sliding out the last word so that she knew exactly what it meant.

"Why did you kill my uncle? What did he ever do to you?"

This time Julie planned her comment, for as soon as she spoke, she crawled backward several feet, hoping to make him think she was in one place when actually she was in another.

"Why, he didn't do nothin' to me, dearie,'' Shardeen replied. "It was just a job, that's all. I was paid to kill him.''

Julie tried to turn around, to go back to the front of the room again, but when she did, she knocked over some more books. They fell with a series of loud thuds, once again giving away her position.

Shardeen fired again, shooting blindly in the direction of the sound. Ironically he was closer this time than he was previously, and Julie could feel the concussion of the bullet whizzing by, frying the air just in front of her before it slammed into the wall.

"If you want, I can kill you first,'' Shardeen said. "Course, I'd like it a little better if you was still alive when we was doin' it, but when you get right down to it, it don't make no never mind to me. Dead or alive, I'll get my pleasure from you.''

From the position of his voice, Julie realized a small glimmer of hope. He was moving aimlessly through the room, which might give her a chance to get out. She started crawling toward the door.

"What you tryin' to do, girl? You think you can make it outside?'' Shardeen asked. He moved again and Julie's heart fell, as she could hear him moving back into a blocking position. "Yeah, you do that. You try an' make it to the door. I'll just be here, waitin' on you.''

Another streak of lightning. The room flashed white, and she could see him standing no more than a few feet from her. Then it grew dark once more, and the thunder boomed.

Driven by terror now, Julie made a desperate run toward the door, but Shardeen anticipated it and in one quick lunge, caught her, then spun her around. In what was almost a reflex action, Julie's hand reached up and clawed at his face. Her long fingernails opened four deep tracks on his face, and he began bleeding.

"Ow! You bitch!" Shardeen shouted. He was still holding his pistol in his hand, and he brought it across the side of her head in a vicious swipe. Julie saw stars flash as the gun barrel struck her in the side of the head, then she went out.

When she came to a few moments later, she was naked, and he was raping her. She could feel him thrusting into her body, tearing at her, sending a searing pain through her almost as if he were using a hot poker. She could hear him squealing over her like a pig, and she was nauseated by the almost overpowering odors: unwashed body, sour beer, tobacco, and spent gunpowder from the two shots he had fired.

Having regained consciousness, Julie began trying to fight him off.

"What? You're still alive? I thought you was dead!" Shardeen said.

Julie tried to twist out from under him.

"Uhmm, yeah, do that," he said. "That makes it better. Oh . . . oh . . . oh!" he moaned, and, with revulsion, Julie realized that he had just finished.

Shardeen pulled himself out of her, then stood up to put himself back inside his pants. He had not even bothered to take his pants down during the rape.

"You just lie there for a moment," Shardeen said. "Soon it'll all be over for you."

My God! He means to kill me as well! Julie thought. So suddenly that her action surprised him, Julie managed to roll over onto her hands and knees. She began crawling quickly, trying to get away from him.

"You ain't goin' nowhere," Shardeen said dryly. Suddenly the inside of the schoolroom was illuminated by another flash of light, only this time it came from inside, not outside, as Shardeen fired his pistol. The gunshot sounded like thunder, and Julie felt something hit her hard in the back, between her shoulder blades.

From a house near the school, a dog began to bark. Shardeen took two quick steps toward Julie's body. Standing over her, he cocked his pistol for a second shot when, outside, more barking dogs joined the first. He thought about it for a moment, then he eased the hammer down and slipped the pistol back into his holster. It wasn't until that moment that he began to feel the pain brought about by Julie's life-and-death struggling scratch. He took his handkerchief out and held it up to the wound.

"Bitch," he snarled. "I was goin' to finish you off . . . make it easy for you. But as far as I'm concerned, you can just lie there and die slow."

With dozens of dogs now adding to the cacophony, Shardeen slipped out of the door, down the steps, then walked, almost casually, across the street to the livery stable. There he mounted his already saddled horse and rode out into the rain, toward the Double-Diamond. He was in no particular hurry. He knew that the chances of anyone coming out in the rain to see what all the dogs were barking about were remote.

BACK INSIDE THE SCHOOLHOUSE, JULIE REGAINED CONsciousness a second time. She tried to get up but couldn't. Slowly and laboriously, she worked her way across the floor to the blackboard wall. Painfully, she reached up to grab the chalk tray and, using it as an assist bar, started pulling herself up. She was almost erect, when she felt her knees weaken and her legs give way. She fell to the floor again.

As she fell, she made a grab to stop the fall, but succeeded only in pulling down a few pieces of chalk.

Julie tried to get up again, but she had no strength left, so she just lay there, feeling herself growing weaker. She began moving her hand around in the dark, on the floor, looking for the chalk. Finally she was able to wrap her fingers around a piece of it and laboriously tried to write something on the floor.

She couldn't hold the chalk . . . she had no strength in her fingers. Twice she started, but she dropped the chalk. Finally, mustering up all the strength and willpower she had remaining, she formed the top part of the first letter.

That was as far as she could go. With strength and will-power gone, her hand trailed away, putting a long, ill-formed tail falling away from the top of the letter.

"I hope I got enough of it," she said. "Please, God," she prayed. "I hope I got enough of it."

18

LATER THAT SAME MORNING, OUT AT THE DOUBLE-Diamond, Cherokee found himself standing on the front porch of the big house, holding his hat in his hand as he waited to speak with Emmerline. It irritated him that the Mexican woman Emmerline had working for him would keep him waiting out on the porch like a panhandler. But he didn't press the issue. He was here to do some business, and he knew that a person couldn't do business if he was argumentative.

Cherokee stepped over to the edge of the porch and looked out over the rolling acres that Emmerline had amassed in the few years he had been here since the war. God, what he wouldn't give to own a place just like this.

Cherokee couldn't help but wonder how Emmerline, who had come to Texas empty-handed after the war, was able to build such a large and impressive ranch in so short a time. Of course it may have helped that Emmerline was a Yankee and knew all the other carpetbaggers. Some said that Emmerline was a Yankee officer during the war, and ex-Yankee officers who knew the right people were able to get things done easier than former Rebs, even Rebs who had been officers.

Cherokee had been an officer, a captain in the Texas Cavalry. When the war ended he returned to Texas hardened and feeling betrayed. Despite the fact that the South had lost the war . . . or perhaps even because of the fact, Cherokee was a man with ambitions. He was going to find some land to homestead, hunt wild cows, and then use the land and cattle as the basis of a ranching empire.

Cherokee had no qualms about what it would take to build his ranch. If he had to throw a long rope now and then, or ride an outlaw trail, then so be it. During the war he had murdered, robbed, pillaged, and burned for the Confederacy. It seemed only right that he should put those well-developed skills to work for himself.

But Cherokee was never able to file the paperwork he needed to take title to the land, and his cow hunts produced only a few miserable specimens, unfit to start a herd. Frustrated by his failure, he finally took a job as foreman for Phillip Wellington.

For a while after starting work for Wellington, Cherokee harbored the secret though totally irrational hope that he and Wellington's daughter might get married. If that would happen, then someday Camelot would belong to him. But he learned very quickly that Pamela Wellington had no interest in him.

With no chance of ever inheriting Camelot, Cherokee's next move was to determine how to convert his position as foreman of the ranch into a means of personal profit. That was the first and only plan of his to come to fruition, when he discovered a secret pass that led to a connecting valley between Camelot and Double-Diamond. It was a valley that, while sheltered from casual observation, could hide several hundred head of cattle.

This presented him with a golden opportunity, but before Cherokee did anything about it, he visited Emmerline and showed him how easily he could convert Camelot's brand, which was a *W* for Wellington, into the brand of two connected diamonds, used by Double-Diamond. He then offered to provide Emmerline with these brand-altered cattle at a bargain price. Emmerline accepted the offer, and for the last six months, Cherokee and Ned, the one cowboy he had recruited from Camelot, rustled cows from Wellington and sold them to Emmerline.

Although that provided Cherokee with an additional source of income, he hit upon another way to make money. Recruiting four out-of-work drifters, men who had served with him during the war, he arranged to have them abduct Pamela Wellington. It was his intention to hold Pamela for a ransom of twenty thousand dollars. That was a small fortune, but he knew that Phillip Wellington not only had that much money, but would readily give it to get his daughter back.

Though he said nothing about it to the men he had recruited, there was a secondary benefit to taking Pamela Wellington prisoner. When Cherokee asked her to go to the Cattlemen's Dance in Loraine, she had laughed at him. Laughed at him, as if he were nothing more than a saddle tramp. As far as Cherokee was concerned, a few days in fear and humiliation would be good for her.

Like his aborted plans to be a large rancher, however, that plan fell apart. Just when things were going well, the Coulters came along—quite by coincidence—and rescued her. Now the Coulter brothers were the fair-haired boys at the ranch. They, and not he, were the ones Phillip Wellington turned to when he wanted something done.

Cherokee had seen the way Pamela Wellington looked at Win Coulter. What did she see in him? He had no better background than Cherokee did. Hell, Win Coulter was a bushwhacker. He had ridden with Quantrill, and everyone knew that Quantrill's Raiders were the wildest and most savage group of men ever to fork a horse.

As far as Cherokee was concerned, Win and Pamela could have each other. It was time to move on. It began to fall apart when the Coulters killed the four men Cherokee had recruited to abduct Pamela. They had been good boys, and they deserved more than to be shot down like mad dogs.

Pete was a good man too, and he deserved better, but Cherokee had had no choice. He hadn't wanted to kill Pete, but Pete caught Cherokee rustling red-handed and was going to tell. Now things were really getting out of hand since

Chad Emmerline had introduced hoof-and-mouth disease onto the range. When Cherokee heard what Emmerline was going to do, he cautioned him against it, but Emmerline didn't listen.

"No, it's perfect if you think about it," Emmerline had said. "One cow put into one isolated herd, and he'll have to destroy every cow on his ranch. That's the law. And there's no way anyone, not even someone as rich as Phillip Wellington, can sustain that kind of loss. He'll wind up losing his land for taxes, and I'll pick it up for a song."

"If you ask me, you're grabbin' a bull by the tail and you might not be able to let go," Cherokee had warned.

Cherokee was right. Emmerline's plan had backfired. Not only did Wellington not have to destroy every animal on his ranch, but Emmerline wound up losing nearly as many of his own cattle. And so did several of the other ranchers.

But, like they say, every cloud has a silver lining, and Cherokee had just found the silver lining to this cloud. He had come here to see Emmerline, to "raise the price of playing poker."

Cherokee's musings were interrupted when, behind him, he heard the front door open and close. He turned to see Emmerline coming out onto the porch.

"What are you doing over here, Cherokee? I told you never to come to my house. This isn't very smart of you," Emmerline growled. "What if someone saw you?"

"I was very careful," Cherokee said. "I came through that hidden pass I told you about. Nobody saw me."

"That doesn't matter. It's not a good idea for you to be seen here. Especially now, with everyone so jittery over this hoof-and-mouth disease thing."

"That's all your own fault, Emmerline. I told you not to do it," Cherokee said. "But you went ahead and put that sick cow in with Mr. Wellington's herd anyway, and look at all the trouble it's caused."

"Yes, well, I guess it turns out that you were right. I certainly didn't expect it to get out of hand the way it did. I thought it would be confined to Camelot. Instead, I wound up havin' to destroy five hundred head of my own cattle."

"I can replace those cows for you," Cherokee offered.

"I'm sure you can, and I'm counting on it," Emmerline said. He smiled. "And the best thing is, the compensation I'm getting for destroying my cows will pay for the replacement. So, if you look at it that way, I'm still way ahead."

Cherokee shook his head. "Well, maybe not quite as far ahead," he said.

"What do you mean? I'm getting five dollars a head for every animal I destroy. And I'm paying you five dollars a head for every cow you bring me. It all comes out in the wash."

"Well, that's what I want to talk to you about. From now on it's goin' to cost you ten dollars a head to replace 'em," Cherokee said.

The smile left Emmerline's face and he looked up sharply. "Ten dollars a head?"

"Ten dollars a head," Cherokee repeated.

"You're getting a little greedy, aren't you?" Emmerline asked.

"I don't call it greedy," Cherokee said. "I call it smart."

"Uh-huh. And what makes you think I'll pay ten dollars a head?"

"Because you need them cows, Mr. Emmerline," Cherokee answered. "You're still gettin' 'em at a bargain rate, and there ain't no place else you can get 'em, 'cept from me. Besides which, you've got no choice. You have to do business with me."

"What do you mean, I have to do business with you?" Emmerline asked.

" 'Cause if you don't . . ." Cherokee paused for a minute and studied the hat he was still turning in his hand, then he cleared his throat. "Well, I just might have to tell some folks how that diseased cow got into the Camelot herd."

"I wouldn't want you to do that, Mr. Brown. That would make things very unpleasant for me," Emmerline said.

"Yes," Cherokee said. "Yes, it would, wouldn't it?"

"Well, Mr. Brown, you have certainly given me something to think about," Emmerline said. "Yes, indeed. I may just have to change the way I do business with you."

Cherokee nodded, then put his hat on, walked out to the hitching rail, and mounted. "I thought you might come around to my way of thinkin', Mr. Emmerline," he said from the saddle.

"I haven't yet," Emmerline said. "But I'll think it over, and I'll send you my answer soon," Emmerline promised.

"Don't make me wait too long, Emmerline," Cherokee said, gaining some confidence now. "I'm sure you wouldn't want me talkin' to the wrong people."

"No," Emmerline said. "I wouldn't want you talking to the wrong people."

Cherokee jerked his horse around, then rode off.

EMMERLINE WATCHED CHEROKEE UNTIL HE WAS OUT OF the gate, then he started toward the guest house to talk to Shardeen. When Emmerline had hired Shardeen, he figured, rightly, that such a person wouldn't do well in the bunkhouse with working cowboys, so he offered him the guest house. Shardeen accepted the offer as if it were his due, though in truth it seemed that he rarely spent his nights there. Sometimes Emmerline would see Shardeen riding out toward town, just before dusk. Then he would see him coming back the next morning at dawn. He didn't know where Shardeen went during those times, nor did he ever inquire.

Last night was such a night. Shardeen had ridden out just after supper, and Emmerline saw him coming back just after breakfast. Did he have a place to stay in town? Or had he spent the night outside, in the rain? Emmerline was curious about it, but he wasn't curious enough to ask questions. As long as Shardeen was around when he needed something done, then he served his purpose. Emmerline certainly had no further use for him.

He did have a use for him now, though, so he stepped up onto the porch of the guest house and knocked on the door.

A moment later Shardeen opened the door.

"My God, what happened to your face?" Emmerline asked when he saw the four deep scratch marks down Shardeen's left cheek.

"I got scratched," Shardeen answered without elaboration.

"I daresay you did."

"You wantin' me to do somethin'?" Shardeen asked. It was obvious he didn't care to talk about the scratches on his face and, therefore, Emmerline didn't mention them again.

"Yes," he said. "I have a little job for you."

AS CHEROKEE RODE BACK TOWARD THE PASS THAT WOULD allow him to go from Double-Diamond to Camelot, he began making plans. They were happy plans. He already had twenty-five hundred dollars put away from his earlier business with Emmerline, and if he brought him five hundred more cows at ten dollars a head, that would be five thousand dollars more. He would have to split with Ned, of course, but he would tell Ned that they were still getting five dollars a head, so Ned's share would only be one thousand two hundred fifty dollars. That would leave Cherokee three thousand seven hundred fifty dollars to add to the poke he already had. With that kind of money he could go anywhere and live like a king. Maybe even California.

Half an hour after he left Emmerline's house, he heard someone coming after him. When he stopped and turned around to look, he saw that it was the albino who worked for Emmerline.

"Well, now, I see it didn't take you long to make up your mind," he said aloud. He chuckled and reached down to pat his horse on the neck. "What do you think, horse? Looks like me an' you's about to be in some pretty tall cotton."

Shardeen pulled up about ten feet away from Cherokee.

You are one ugly son of a bitch, Cherokee thought, though he didn't give voice to the words. Then he noticed the four long, red marks on Shardeen's left cheek. Because they were so dark against his milk-white skin, Cherokee thought for a moment that he had painted his face, like an Indian, and he studied them in curiosity. Then he saw, quite clearly, that they were scratch marks.

"Ha, look at them scratch marks!" Cherokee said.

"What'd you do, run into a woman who didn't want anything to do with you?"

Shardeen put his hand to the scratch marks for a second, then lowered it.

"You might say that," he said.

"Oooweee. Seems to me like that's more woman than you can handle. If I was you, I'd stay away from her."

"I won't be seeing her again."

"So, what are you doing out here? Were you coming for me?"

"Yes."

"Emmerline sent you?"

"Yes."

Cherokee smiled broadly. "Yeah, I figured he'd see things my way. What did he tell you?"

"He told me to kill you."

The smile froze on Cherokee's face. For just a moment he wasn't sure he'd heard what he thought he heard. Then he thought it must be some sort of joke, though it was a joke that made his skin tingle.

"That . . . that ain't funny," Cherokee said nervously.

"No, I don't reckon it is," Shardeen replied. He pulled his pistol and pointed it at Cherokee.

"What the—" Cherokee shouted. "No, wait! Wait! Tell Emmerline I was just—"

Shardeen pulled the trigger and the slug caught Cherokee in the center of his chest, right in the breastbone. It hit with the impact of a hammer, and Cherokee felt all the breath leave his body. He put his hands over the entry wound, then looked down to watch in horror as his own bright red blood began spilling through his fingers. He tried hard to stay in the saddle, but lost the struggle when Shardeen fired a second time. That bullet hit Cherokee right between the eyes.

19

MICHAEL GUNN WAS NOT ONLY A LAWYER, OR "BARRIS-ter," as Wellington liked to say, he was also the father of two school-aged children and the president of the Loraine school board. When Miss Lulu Belle Carmody resigned her position to get married, Gunn was charged with the responsibility of finding a replacement teacher. It was Phillip Wellington's recommendation that Gunn hire Miss Julie Vincent for the upcoming school year.

"Julie Vincent is an exceptionally bright young lady," Wellington had said, "and someone who is at ease with responsibility. And she is also a very pretty young woman, as you shall soon see. I don't think the school board will have any regrets."

"I would hope she is not too pretty," Gunn had replied. "Miss Carmody was rather plain, yet even she managed to get married. The pretty ones don't last long at all. Sometimes they get married in the middle of the school year, and if that happens, we are left in a terrible fix."

Gunn, with the approval of the school board, hired Julie Vincent for the upcoming school year. Classes would be starting on Monday morning, and last week Julie had moved into her room behind the school. She had spent the entire previous week getting ready.

Shortly after Julie arrived, she gave Michael Gunn a list

of repairs she wished made to the school. One request was that the roof be repaired, and, because of the heavy rain yesterday and last night, Gunn decided to go over to the schoolhouse today to see for himself how badly the roof leaked.

He was surprised to find the front door of the school standing wide open. He climbed the steps, then stuck his head in through the door.

"Miss Vincent?" he called. "Miss Vincent, it is I, Michael Gunn. Did you intend to leave the door open?"

When Gunn got no response from his call, he took another few steps into the schoolroom. "Miss Vincent, are you here?" he called. He looked around the room and saw several books lying on the floor.

"My word," he said. "What is all this?"

Miss Vincent had only been here a few days, but already Gunn had been impressed with her neatness and organization. It certainly wasn't like her to leave books lying around. How strange, he thought.

"Miss Vincent?" he repeated.

Gunn moved farther into the room, then stepped on a piece of cloth. Curious as to what it could be, and what it was doing on the floor, he reached down to pick it up.

It was a nightgown. And, more shocking, it was covered with blood! Something was wrong. Something was terribly, terribly wrong.

"Miss Vincent?" Gunn called, his voice louder and more urgent.

Gunn moved to the front of the classroom, which was actually the back of the school building. When he reached the first row of desks, he saw something that had been previously blocked from his view by those same desks. There on the floor halfway between her own desk and the blackboard lay Julie Vincent.

"My God!" Gunn gasped.

Totally naked, the teacher was lying on her stomach, with an ugly, black bullet hole in her back, between her shoulder blades. Her head was turned to one side, and her eyes were open and unseeing. Her right arm was outstretched, and a piece of chalk lay on the floor beside her hand.

WIN AND JOE WERE FITTING PIPE TO ONE OF THE WELLS when Eb rode up.

"Hi, Eb," Joe greeted with a smile. He took in the well with a wave of his hand. "What do you think? We'll have this one going by the end of the day. That will give Camelot five working wells."

"Yeah, it looks good," Eb said. His voice was low and solemn.

"What is it?" Win asked. "What's wrong?"

Eb took a deep breath. "Don't know no way to say this, other'n to come right out an' say it," he began. "Joe, you know that girl that was here for a while? The Vincent girl?"

"Julie, yes, what about her?" Joe asked.

"Well, Joe, I hate to be the one to tell you this, seein' as how I think you was maybe a little sweet on her."

"What is it, Eb?"

Eb took his hat off and ran his hand through his hair.

"They found her dead this mornin'," Eb said. "That is, Lawyer Gunn, he found her dead."

"What? Where? How?"

"She was lyin' on the floor in the schoolhouse. The talk is, she must've been raped," Eb said. "She was naked, and she had a bullet hole in her back."

"Oh, damn," Joe said with a long, breath-expelling sigh. "What kind of a bastard would hurt a sweet girl like that?"

"Have they caught who did it?" Win asked.

Eb shook his head. "They don't even know who did it," he said. "But whoever it was, his name starts with a C."

Joe looked up in interest. "His name starts with a C? How do you know that?"

" 'Cause before she died she wrote the letter C on the floor of the school," Eb explained. "They figure she must've been trying to write the name of whoever did it, but that there letter C is as far as she got."

Joe started for his horse. "I'm going into town, Win," he said.

"I figured you would."

Joe mounted, then looked back toward his brother. "Well, you comin' with me, or not?"

"I'm comin'," Win replied.

ELY PRUFROCK, THE TOWN UNDERTAKER, HAD LEARNED his trade during the war. He became so skilled at restoring battle-damaged soldiers to a state to be viewed by their grieving family members that he achieved a well-deserved degree of fame. Now, when he had a project of which he was particularly proud, he would display the body on a catafalque just inside the big glass window on the front of his funeral home.

He was particularly proud of the job he had done with Julie Vincent. He had fixed her face into a slight smile, used rouge and lip paint to restore some color, and combed her hair so that it lay in soft curls around her face.

Since her uncle was killed just a short time earlier, Julie Vincent had no family to view her. Prufrock thought it would be a shame to let such a wonderful job pass without some recognition, so he lay her body in his most beautiful coffin, a black lacquer box with silver scrollwork. Then, folding her arms across her chest, he placed a single yellow rose in her hands and put her on the catafalque in the front of his establishment.

Word began to spread around town that Julie's body would soon be on display. As a result, a crowd gathered outside the window. Some were friends, here out of genuine grief. Some were mothers and fathers of the children Julie was to have taught, and they were here out of respect. But a sizable number had gathered from unashamed curiosity.

As if opening the curtain on a staged drama, Ely Prufrock pulled back the drapes so his work could be seen. Then he stepped outside, beaming proudly, as he listened to the accolades for his work.

"Oh, look how beautiful she is," someone said.

"Doesn't she look natural?"

"The color's good."

"Just like she's sleepin'."

WHEN THE COULTER BROTHERS ARRIVED AT ABOUT THAT time, they saw the crowd gathered around Prufrock's front window, and they rode over to see what everyone was looking at. They were startled to see Julie's body, and, because Joe didn't want to see her this way, he jerked the horse away quickly.

"Let's get the hell away from here," he growled.

"Good idea," Win agreed. "What do you say we go down to the saloon and have a drink?"

"Yeah. Well, I'll be there in a couple of minutes," Joe replied. "First, I want to go down to the schoolhouse and have a look around."

"All right," Win said. "I'll see you in a bit."

When Joe reached the school building, he saw two men, wearing badges, standing out front. He dismounted and started inside.

"Where do you think you're a'goin'?" one of the deputies asked.

"Inside," Joe replied, pointing to the door. "I want to see where she was killed."

"Mister, you want to gander, you go down there with the rest of 'em and look through the window at Prufrock's. They got the little lady on display down there. No need in your hangin' around here. There ain't nothin' to see."

"Wait a minute, Bill," the other deputy said, when he noticed the pained look on Joe's face. "Did you know her, mister?"

"Yes," Joe answered without elaboration.

"Come on, Bill. Let him go on inside, it ain't goin' to hurt nothin'."

"Lennie, you heard what the sheriff said, same as me. He said, don't let nobody mess up what she wrote on the floor."

"We'll go inside with him," Lennie suggested. "He won't mess nothin' up."

"What's your name, anyway?" the deputy called Bill asked.

"Coulter. Joe Coulter."

"Coulter?" Bill replied, putting his finger alongside his nose. "Is that Coulter with a C or with a K?"

"C."

"That's interestin'," Bill said. "Come on inside, and I'll show you why."

Joe and the two deputies went into the empty school building. Bill pointed to a chalk mark on the floor. "We figure she must've been tryin' to tell us who killed her," he explained. "Only thing is, she died before she could get it writ. All she could make was the letter C. Like the C that's in your name," he added pointedly.

"You think I did it?"

"Nope," Bill replied easily. "If I thought you done it, I'd have my gun out an' pointin' at you by now. But I know you didn't because," he put his hand to his face, "you ain't marked up none."

"What do you mean?"

"It seems that when Mr. Prufrock examined the girl's body he found blood and skin under her fingernails. He reckons Miss Vincent must've put up a pretty good fight before she was shot in the back."

"You mean she was shot in the back?"

"Sure was. It's a cowardly thing to do to anyone, but I think it is particular bad when someone shoots a woman in the back."

"Sure would like to get my hands on the son of a bitch who did it," Lennie said.

"Yeah, me too," Bill agreed. "I'll tell you one thing, if we do catch him and a crowd gathers outside the jail to lynch him, I sure as hell ain't goin' to be the one that fights 'em off."

Joe thanked the two deputies for letting him look around, then rode over to the Black Horse Saloon. He tied his horse off at the same hitching post Win used so that the horses, used to each other by now, would stand quietly side by side, then he went inside. Win was already at the bar, and

Joe went over to stand beside him. The bartender put a mug of beer in front of him before he could even speak.

"I already ordered, and I told him to be on the lookout for you," Win explained.

The two brothers, their drinks in their hands, turned their backs to the bar and looked out over the other patrons. It was pretty clear what the conversation was about. Everyone was talking about the "beautiful young schoolmarm," who was found on the floor of the schoolhouse. And there were as many speculations as to what happened to her as there were speculators.

Joe was just finishing his beer when Shardeen pushed his way into the saloon through the batwing doors. His entrance had an immediate chilling effect on the patrons, and though all conversations didn't stop, they did grow much less animated.

"I wish that son of a bitch would find some other place to do his drinkin'," the bartender growled. "Ever'time he comes in here, my business drops off."

"Why?" Win asked.

"Don't you know? That's Lucas Shardeen. He's the one killed them two cowboys from the Cripple C, for no reason a'tall. He just up an' picked a fight with 'em, then shot 'em down in cold blood."

"We were told it was a fair fight," Win said.

"Fair fight? Look at him, the way he wears his guns kicked out like that," the bartender replied. "You think anyone could get the better of him in a fair fight?"

Shardeen stood in the door for just a moment, looking over the patrons in the saloon, then he turned and walked over to the far end of the bar. The patrons who had been standing there moved away, giving him a wide berth. That was when Joe saw his face. And what he saw made him draw in a quick, audible breath.

"What is it?" Win asked quietly.

Joe didn't answer. Instead, he dipped his finger into his beer, then began marking on the bar. First he made the letter C. Then he made the letter S. Then he started to make the letter S, but he didn't complete it. Instead, he let his

finger tail away. The result was a mark that looked exactly
like the chalk mark Julie had left on the floor over at the
school.

"Son of a bitch!" Joe said under his breath. "It isn't a
C, it's an S!"

"What are you talking about?"

"The mark Julie left on the floor. Ever'one thinks it is
a letter C. But it ain't." He pointed to his own effort, which
was already beginning to dry up. "It's an S that she
couldn't finish, just like that one."

"S? Shardeen?"

Joe nodded. "Look at his face. The deputies said she
scratched whoever did it. He did it, Win. There ain't a
doubt in my mind. Shardeen killed Julie Vincent."

Joe started toward Shardeen. Anxious for him, Win
reached out to put his hand on his brother's shoulder.

"Easy, Joe," he said. "You've heard the talk about him.
He's damned good with that gun. I'm not sure I could even
handle him."

"You won't have to handle him," Joe replied quietly.
"I'll do it."

"Joe?" Win started anxiously, but paying no attention
whatever to his brother, Joe went over to stand beside Shardeen.

Shardeen, not used to being crowded, looked up.

"Step back, you big bastard," he said. "I don't like
bein' crowded."

"Did you kill Julie Vincent?"

"What?" Shardeen asked, not only surprised by the
question, but surprised that anyone would have the nerve
to ask it.

"Julie Vincent," Joe repeated. "Did you kill her? Is that
how you got those scratches on your face?"

Shardeen put his hand to his cheek. "I got these here
scratches by ridin' through some brambles," he said.

"You're a lyin' son of a bitch, Shardeen. Julie scratched
you when you killed her."

"You can't prove that."

"Prove it? I don't have to prove it, you maggoty bastard. All I have to do is believe it."

No one had ever challenged Shardeen like this, and there was a collective gasp of breath as everyone started paying close attention to the conversation between Joe and Shardeen.

"Mister, I'm going to count to three," Shardeen hissed. "If you ain't gone by then, you'd better be drawin' your gun, 'cause I'm going to blow a hole through your innards."

By now, even those who had gone upstairs had somehow learned what was going on, and several of them came to the railing on the second-floor landing. They stood there, like patrons in a theater, looking down on the drama that was playing out at the bar. A few looked at the clock to note the time. They would need all the facts for their telling and retelling of the story over the years.

"Start counting, you runty little son of a bitch," Joe said.

Now not only conversation but breathing stopped as everyone waited, silently, to see what was going to happen. The loudest sound in the room was the measured ticktock of the pendulum clock that stood on the side wall between the piano and a brass spittoon.

An evil smile spread across Shardeen's lips. He liked the old adage: The bigger they are, the harder they fall. This son of a bitch was big, and he was going to fall like an oak tree.

"One," Shardeen started.

Joe didn't flinch.

"Two . . . three . . ." At three, Shardeen drew his pistol. He expected to see Joe going for his own gun, but Joe surprised him. Instead of attempting to draw against Shardeen, Joe stuck his hand out and intercepted Shardeen's hand as it came up.

This was the same hand Shardeen had wrapped around the handle of his pistol. It was small, delicate, and graceful. . . . all desirable attributes for someone who wanted to learn the skill of rapidly drawing and firing a pistol.

But the pliant fragility that was an advantage to the

skilled shootist now became a shortcoming. Joe squeezed his big hand down on Shardeen's small one.

"Hey, what the hell?" Shardeen shouted.

Joe squeezed hard, so hard that Shardeen's fingers began breaking one by one.

"Ahhhh!" Shardeen screamed in pain as he felt his fingers snap under Joe's viselike grip.

The evil and confident smile on Shardeen's face was instantly replaced by an expression of pain and surprise.

Joe began to raise Shardeen's hand. Shardeen had no idea what Joe had in mind, but he was powerless to prevent it. Shardeen's gun hand came up, then twisted around backward. As the muzzle of his own pistol was brought around to bear on his face, Shardeen's expression of pain and surprise turned to one of awareness and horror.

"No!" Shardeen screamed. "No, what are you doing?"

At that moment it became impossible for him to speak further, because Joe rammed the barrel of Shardeen's own pistol down his mouth. He thrust the gun barrel so far down Shardeen's throat that Shardeen started gagging.

That was when Joe pulled the trigger.

20

THE GLEAMING COACH AND FOUR STOOD ON THE CURVING driveway in front of Wellington's house. The driver stood on the ground beside it with the door open. Win and Joe, their horses saddled, were waiting as well, for Wellington had asked them if they would go into town with him.

"You're certain you don't want to ride in the coach?" he asked as he started to get in.

"No, thanks," Win replied. "I feel closed up in those things."

Wellington chuckled. "A bit of claustrophobia, eh? Well, I suppose I can understand the condition, though, believe me, it is much more comfortable riding on a padded seat than sitting on a hard saddle."

"I'll grant you that," Win replied.

"I want to thank you two men for going to see the federal inspector with me," Wellington said. "You can give him a firsthand report on the disastrous effect that Gypsum River dam has had."

"We'll be glad to tell him our story, Mr. Wellington," Win said. "But I don't know how much attention a Yankee government official is going to pay to the likes of us."

"Oh, he'll pay a good deal of attention, I should think. Especially when he learns that Joe is a water engineer."

Joe laughed. "A water engineer, am I? Well, I would've never called myself such a thing."

"And why not? Have you, or have you not, located and dug five producing water wells?"

"Well, I've done that, I reckon," Joe agreed.

"That, my fine friend, makes you a water engineer," Wellington said. Just before he got into the coach, he saw Eb giving some of the cowboys their instructions for today. "Still no sign of Mr. Brown?" he asked.

Win shook his head. "I've checked around," he said. "No one has seen hide nor hair of Cherokee in nearly a week."

"How very odd that he should just disappear like that," Wellington said.

"That's the way it is with some men," Win said. "When they get the urge to move on, that's just what they do."

"Yes, well, I do wish he would have had the common courtesy to tell me that he was leaving. That way I could've found a new foreman."

As they were talking, the cowboys who had been instructed by Eb started to ride away. One of them stopped and called a question back to Eb. Eb answered it to the cowboy's satisfaction, and the cowboy nodded, then rode on.

"Seems to me like you've already found your new foreman," Win said. "Eb seems to be running things better'n Cherokee ever did."

Wellington had been watching Eb as well, and he nodded. "Yes, I am quite pleased with the way Eb has stepped in and taken over. I think you might be right about him," he agreed.

Wellington got into the coach then, and the driver closed the door, then climbed up onto the high box that was his seat. With a whistle and a snap of the lines, the team lurched forward and the coach began to roll out of the driveway, the gravel making a crunching sound under the steel-rimmed wheels.

● ● ●

WHEN THEY REACHED TOWN, THEY WENT DIRECTLY TO the law offices of Morton, Tregailian, and Gunn. Gunn met them on the front porch, then they all went to lunch at Maxine's Cafe.

"Mr. Hinsdale is due to arrive at two o'clock," Gunn explained over the lunch table. "We will meet his train and talk to him long enough to make our grievances known, then we'll go see Canby."

"Do you really think you're goin' to get any satisfaction from a damned Yankee official?" Joe asked.

"This Yankee is from Washington," Gunn explained. "It is to be hoped that we would get a fairer judgment from him than we would from some carpetbagger."

"Like that pissant Canby, you mean?" Joe said.

"My point exactly," Gunn replied. "If Canby has been unduly influenced by the likes of someone like Chad Emmerline, then we have recourse in the court system."

A SMALL MAN WEARING A THREE-PIECE SUIT AND GLASSES which were supported not by earpieces but by perching on the end of his nose stepped down from the train. A gold chain stretched across his vest, and he pulled his watch out and examined it.

"Would you be Mr. Abner Hinsdale?" Gunn asked, stepping up to the arriving passenger.

"I am, sir. And you would be Mr. Canby?"

"No, I am Michael Gunn. I represent Mr. Wellington and some of the other area ranchers."

"Ah, yes," Hinsdale replied. "You are the lawyer who has filed a petition to halt the water improvement project."

"Yes," Gunn said. "But I am also the lawyer who requested the water improvement project in the first place."

"Mr. Gunn, you must realize that a government project is rather like a steamboat paddling down a river. Once it is in motion, it takes a great deal of effort to stop it, or to turn it around. So tell me, why the change of heart?"

"The dam," Gunn said.

Hinsdale looked confused. "The dam? What dam? We authorized no dam."

Gunn and Wellington looked at each other in surprise, then Gunn turned back to Hinsdale.

"Are you telling me that the government did not authorize a dam to be built across Gypsum River?"

"Heavens no. Why would we do that?" Hinsdale asked. "I've studied the maps. A dam across Gypsum River could create water deprivation for the entire range."

"It not only could, it has," Gunn said. "For indeed, Mr. Hinsdale, a dam has been built."

"Does Mr. Canby know about this?"

"Indeed he does, Mr. Hinsdale, for he is the one who built it," Wellington said.

Hinsdale took his glasses from the end of his nose and polished them furiously for a moment, then he put them back on.

"Gentlemen," he said, squaring his shoulders. "I suggest we go speak with Mr. Canby. If what you are telling me is true, he has some explaining to do."

During the walk from the railroad depot to Canby's office, Gunn told Hinsdale about some of the water problems the range had been facing lately, and how those problems had been exacerbated by the dam across Gypsum River.

"The problem has been somewhat alleviated by the engineering genius of Mr. Joe Coulter," Wellington put in.

"Oh? And what has Mr. Coulter done?" Hinsdale asked.

"He is getting water from underground," Wellington said.

"I see. You have located and identified the aquifer, then?"

"The what?" Joe asked.

"The aquifer . . . the underground source of water. I thought you were an engineer."

"I never said that," Joe said.

"Then how did you find the water?"

"I witched it, with a dowser," Joe said easily.

Hinsdale laughed. "You found the water by dowsing for it? How quaint."

"It might be quaint, Mr. Hinsdale, but Camelot now has five good wells and is much less dependent upon Gypsum

River. Still, the dam must be removed if the other ranchers are to get their fair share of water.''

At that moment they reached the district water office. The door was standing slightly ajar, and Hinsdale pushed it open.

''I shall be interested in hearing what Mr. Canby has to say about this,'' Hinsdale said, stepping into the office. ''Canby?'' he called. ''Canby, it is Abner Hinsdale, from the Department of the Interior. Are you here?''

There was an eerie silence to the office, and the four visitors stood there for a moment, waiting for Canby's reply.

''He should be here,'' Hinsdale said. ''I am absolutely positive he knew that today was the day I was to arrive.''

''He knew it,'' Gunn said. ''We were talking about it last night.'' Gunn pushed through a little spring-loaded gate that separated the front of the office from the rear. ''There's a document storage room in the back,'' he said. ''Perhaps he's back there.''

''If what you gentlemen have told me about the dam is true, it's going to take more than a few documents to justify his action,'' Hinsdale said, pushing through the gate to follow Gunn to the back.

Gunn opened the door, then stopped short, with a look of surprise on his face. ''I'll be damned,'' he said.

''What is it, Michael?'' Wellington asked.

Gunn stepped back, then pointed toward the open door. ''Canby is in there,'' he said.

Knowing that something was wrong, Win, Joe, and Wellington moved through the little gate to join Hinsdale, who was also now looking through the door, his mouth open in surprise.

There, hanging from a rafter, twisting slowly at the end of a rope, was the body of Harper Canby.

WIN, JOE, WELLINGTON, HINSDALE, AND A UNITED STATES marshal were riding out to the dam. There, Hinsdale would order the sluices opened immediately, thus providing a source of water for all the ranches downstream. Then he would make the determination as to whether or not the dam itself should be brought down.

There was no longer a question about the legality of the dam. Canby's suicide note explained it all. He told how he had accepted money from Emmerline to use the water improvement project to both enrich the Double-Diamond and to impoverish all the other ranches.

The letter also gave one piece of additional information, information which Win and Joe could scarcely believe.

"In the interest of truth, and the hope that such disclosure will, somehow, make amends for my own transgressions, I would also inform you that the man you know as Chad Emmerline is in fact Felix Parnell, late a captain in the Federal Army. A few months after the war ended, Captain Parnell stole an army payroll with which he had been entrusted, and deserted. That stolen payroll provided the money he needed to start his ranch."

"Felix Parnell?" Win said in surprise.

"You have heard of him?" Wellington asked.

"Yes," Win said. "If it is the same one, I have heard of him."

"Win, how can it be the same one?" Joe asked. "The Felix Parnell that we know is dead."

"Is he?" Win asked.

"You know he is," Joe said. "We killed him!"

"We thought we did," Win agreed. "But, if you recall, we didn't stay around long enough to make certain. We never saw his body."

"We didn't have to see the body. How could anyone live through something like that?"

"We did, Little Brother," Win replied easily.

Joe was silent for a long moment, then he nodded. "Yeah," he said. "Yeah, that's true, isn't it? We did live through it."

"From the tone of the discussion you two are having, I gather that you know Emmerline from before," Wellington said.

"I don't know," Win answered. "We knew a Captain

Felix Parnell. But the man we knew sure didn't look anything at all like Emmerline.''

''You are no doubt talking about his lack of hair,'' Wellington said. ''He explained that to me once. It seems that, during the war, he was caught in a terrible explosion. The effect of the explosion was not only to burn off all the hair on his head, but also to destroy the follicles that grow hair.''

''Son of a bitch,'' Win said. ''It *is* the same one. It has to be.''

''Tell me about him,'' Wellington said, riding alongside them, the better to hear the story.

Win explained that Felix Parnell had been a captain in the Federal Army, and a particular adversary during the war. As provost marshal for Kansas City, Captain Parnell was the one who was charged with the responsibility of rounding up Quantrill and all of his Raiders, including men like Bloody Bill Anderson, George Todd, Frank and Jesse James, the Younger brothers, and Win and Joe Coulter.

But Quantrill and his Raiders were proving to be too elusive for him, so Parnell decided to give himself some leverage. He did that by rounding up all the wives, sisters, mothers, daughters, and sweethearts of the men fighting for the South and putting them in a makeshift prison over a liquor store in Kansas City.

The conditions in the women's temporary prison were as harsh as any prisoner-of-war camp in the country. In addition, there were no provisions made for the fact that these particular prisoners were of the ''gentler'' sex.

The women were watched over by armed guards, publicly humiliated, and physically mistreated. And, when a tornado struck Kansas City, Captain Parnell made no effort to move them to a safer place. As a result, many of them, including Bloody Bill Anderson's sister and a girl Joe was particularly fond of, were killed.

Later, when the war was over and Joe and Win, responding to a general offer of amnesty, turned themselves in, Captain Felix Parnell took it upon himself to deny them the parole that had been granted to everyone else. It was his intention to take personal charge of Win and Joe, and to escort them to St. Louis where he planned to publicly hang them.

But Parnell underestimated the ingenuity of the Coulter brothers. In a daring escape, the boys ignited a keg of gunpowder which was being carried on the same train that was transporting them to St. Louis. Railroad regulations directed that both the prisoners and the powder be carried in a special car attached to the end of the train.

The explosion not only separated the car from the rest of the train, it blew the car apart. Win and Joe, who were in the rear, managed to duck down behind the seats and thus avoid the blast. Then, with the car blown free from the train and in smithereens about them, they were able to get away.

Captain Felix Parnell and the escorting guards were in the front part of the car during the explosion. Until today, Win and Joe had thought the guards and Parnell had been killed in the blast. It would appear, however, that somehow Parnell had survived.

EMMERLINE WAS STANDING AT THE SLUICE GATE WHEN they arrived. Word had already reached him that Canby had committed suicide, and Emmerline reasoned, correctly, that there would be a note implicating him. He jacked a shell into his rifle and held it out in front of him.

"That's far enough," he called. He was smoking a cigar, and he pulled the cigar from his mouth to use as a pointer. "You can just turn around and go on back to town."

"Mr. Emmerline, this gentleman with us is Abner Hinsdale," Wellington said. "He is a representative of the Federal Department of the Interior. He has come to order the sluice to be opened so that the water may flow."

"I don't give a damn if he is the President of the United States," Emmerline replied. "Nobody is going to touch my dam."

"Oh, so it has become *your* dam now, has it?" Wellington asked. "Well, I am glad you have given up the charade of saying it was a project backed by the government.''

Win rode up a little closer, in order to get a really good look.

"I'll be a son of a bitch," he said. "Joe, it's true. It is him."

"You mean he *is* Captain Parnell?" Joe asked.

"Yes," Win replied. He looked at Parnell. "Do you remember us?"

"The Coulter brothers. You may as well ask me if I remember Quantrill, George Todd, or Bloody Bill Anderson. In fact, I have even more of a reason for remembering you two bastards," Parnell said. "You thought you killed me, didn't you? You left me there to die. Only I didn't die. Instead, I came out looking like this."

Parnell waved his hand in front of his face, then laughed. "At first, I was angry. But later, it proved to be a blessing in disguise. When I stole the payroll money they posted a reward for Felix Parnell. But Felix Parnell no longer existed, you see. He really *did* die in that train explosion."

"Mr. Parnell, it's all over for you now."

Parnell shook his head. "No," he said. "I told you, Parnell is dead. Don't you know who you are talking to? I am Chad Emmerline. I am one of the biggest ranchers in the state of Texas. Why, I can buy and sell people like you!"

"No you can't, and that's the point," Hinsdale said. "I have already taken steps to have the federal government confiscate your ranch. And you, Mr. Parnell, are going to prison for robbery and for bribing a government official."

"Step aside, Parnell," the U.S. marshal called. "Step aside so we can open the sluice gates."

"You want the sluice gates open?" Parnell said. "I'll accommodate you."

Parnell twisted around and touched the lit end of his cigar to a fuse.

"I'm blowing this dam all to hell! You want water? You'll get water!" Parnell shouted.

A quick glance around showed Win the danger they were in. They were in the dry riverbed, but just on the other side of the dam was a lake, caused by the pooling of the river. When the dam went, a thirty-foot-high wall of water would come crashing down on them. Here, the sides were too steep and too high to get out. It was at least fifty yards back down the riverbed before the sides sloped gently enough to allow them to exit.

"Let's get out of here!" Win shouted, turning his horse around even as he called the warning.

Parnell began laughing hysterically. "Run! Run, you lily-livered bastards! Run!"

Win sensed his brother to one side of him. To his surprise, Wellington managed to get ahead of them, taking his horse over obstacles as easily as if he were running on a road. The marshal was just behind, and Hinsdale was behind the marshal.

The blast went off then. Win felt it before he heard it—a pressure wave that washed over him from the rear like a hot, desert wind. Shortly after that he heard it, a deep-throated roar as loud as any explosion he had ever experienced during the war.

He reached the sloping sides of the riverbed and with the slightest touch turned his horse. The horse responded quickly and within a few bounds they were out of danger.

Turning back toward the riverbed he saw the wall of water crashing down through the channel, knocking down trees, sweeping up debris, tumbling and swirling with so much energy that even the sides of the river were caving in.

Hinsdale's horse stumbled as it started up the side and he was thrown over its head. Joe, who was the closest, darted down to him, then leaned over from saddle, reached down, and, with one hand, was able to snap the small man up. He rode back to the safety of the others, just as the water came crashing through where Hinsdale had been. Hinsdale's horse wasn't as lucky, and Win saw its eyes, wide in terror, as it was swept helplessly downstream.

AFTER THE WATER WENT DOWN, ITS LEVEL LOWERED BY the fact that it was now furnishing water for the entire valley, they found Parnell's body. It was lying on the side of the river, half in and half out. His neck was broken.

Joe and Win stood just over his body, looking down at it for a few moments, then they climbed back up the bank and mounted their horses. Wellington and the others had already started east, toward Camelot, and were at least a quarter of a mile away by now. The Coulters looked in their direction.

"Win, did you leave anything back at the ranch?" Joe asked.

"Nothing I can't replace," Win answered.

"Which way?"

"West."

"Sounds good to me."